"The Battleship Church"

From Bootcamp to Battlefield

by
Joshua

Table of Contents

Introduction

First, I want to start by saying that I am not a writer. I have never had any interest in writing a book. I took the time to write this book because of what God did during this series that literally transformed our church family forever. And if God can use this book to do the same in your life or your church, then this book is worth writing.

A little about myself: I grew up in the church (a preacher's kid), but I was really turned off by many things that happened in the church. At the age of thirteen, I chose not to be serious about the church, God, or following Jesus. I got in with the punk rock scene, skateboarding, doing drugs, and rebelling against almost everything. Until I was nineteen, I was living a normal party lifestyle. I got married during high school, but at this point, I had lost the trust of my wife, who was pregnant at the time, and I was headed down the road of destruction. In the summer of 2005, at a kids' camp in Columbus, Texas, I gave my life to Jesus. Over the next ten months, he restored my marriage. We had our first son, Rylin, and God called me to preach the Gospel.

I didn't know what that looked like. I got saved at a Children's Church Camp. I had a great relationship with the Children's Church pastor, so I started in Children's Church, which seems like forever ago. Over the next ten years, I worked in children's ministry, led youth ministry at two different churches, and Pastored Onalaska First Assembly of God for two years. In 2015, I returned to the church where ministry started for me, Clawson Church in Pollok, Texas. I became the Lead Pastor in March of 2017 and will celebrate seven years of leading this church family in five months. I hope I am here forever.

At Clawson, under my leadership, we attract two main groups of people: unreached people who may have never been open to the Gospel before and people whom the church has hurt. Being in the Bible belt in East Texas, we struggle a lot in the church world down here with a religious, legalistic spirit that pushes people out of church and away from Christ. A lot of churches are very Pharisee and Sadducee-minded, and because of that, they have hurt the church in many ways. With that being said, our church tries to serve as a beacon of light in the area for people who are not interested in the church.

That is just a little bit about me and my church family. Now, I would like to understand why I believe this book's information is important enough for you to take the time to read it.

All this year, God has been speaking to me about the importance of the empowerment of the church.

Matthew 16:18-19 New King James Version

"18 And I also say to you that you are Peter, and on this rock, I will build My church, and the gates of Hades shall not[a]prevail against it. 19 And I will give you the keys of the kingdom of heaven, and whatever you bind on earth [b]will be bound in heaven, and whatever you loose on earth will be loosed in heaven."

The gates of Hell shall not prevail against the church. This means that the Church of Jesus Christ should push back the darkness to attack the enemy! We should push back the gates of Hell as we are offensively attacking. Maybe I am wrong, but that is not a picture I see whenever I look at churches worldwide today. The image that I have in mind is more like the enemy is attacking the church, and the church is attempting to defend itself. Instead of us pushing back the gates of Hell, we are getting our butts kicked by the enemy.

So, the year 2023 at Clawson has been all about God empowering the church through the Holy Spirit to aggressively push back the darkness instead of getting our butts kicked. How do we start kicking the butt of the enemy? Back in August, as we were getting ready for our upcoming Miracle Night, I felt like the Lord spoke into my spirit, "It is time for War." I shared that with our church family and partnering churches on Miracle Night. I declared war against the Kingdom of Darkness.

Well, I don't know if you have ever declared war against Satan before. Let me tell you from experience: if you declare war against Satan and his army, it is probably a good idea to make sure that you and your army are ready to fight. Needless to say, I declared war before we were prepared to fight.

I, pastor of a church, don't lead an army, or at least I thought I didn't. September was a crazy month. First, I had declared war against the kingdom of darkness, so attack after attack came from the enemy, and we were not ready to handle it.

The series of messages I preached in September was titled "Fool's Gold." It was all about realizing the things in our lives that we have viewed as valuable that hold no eternal value whatsoever: money and stuff, fame and power, sex, drugs, rock 'n roll, approval of people, and comfort. I didn't know that God was using this series to refocus our church and get things out of our lives to prepare us for War.

On Thursday, September 21, I was meeting for an hour of prayer with Brett and Jeremy (a couple of pastors I pray with on Thursdays). While we were praying, one of them said, "The most valuable thing on this planet is a human soul, so much so that heaven and hell war over them daily." At that moment, the Lord spoke to my spirit, "Josh, I want you to join in that war."

We were set to start a series called "The Battleship Church" in the first week of October. I wrote this series because we have a value at Clawson that says, "Our Church is a battleship, not a cruise ship." I was going to preach a series over that value. I had no idea what God was putting together for this series and how he was about to transform our church into an Army for Jesus.

The following six chapters are the messages preached to our church family during this series. I think these messages should be shared with the army of Christ worldwide. We took over 260 people through six weeks of boot camp. I text them at 6 am every morning for spiritual boot camp training. Those text messages are all written in each chapter. Chapter eight is some of the testimonies we begin to receive from people going through the boot camp.

If you allow him to, God will use this book to change your life personally as you join the war, go through boot camp, and become a soldier in the army of Christ. Or, if you are a pastor or a church leader, I would like to invite you to pray and consider taking your church through this training and spiritual boot camp. I challenge you to watch how God will transform your church into an Army for Christ.

Please do not hesitate to reach out if I can help you in any way.

Pastor Josh Poage
Clawson Church
www.Clawson.TV
Joshpoage@yahoo.com

Week 1

"Defining the Fight"

Kristi Poage:

Good morning, Clawson family. We are so pumped and ready to kick off this series of messages God has been putting in our hearts. Josh and I have been talking a lot about the state of the church of Jesus worldwide, especially in the American Church. We feel in our spirits that God is saying it is time for His church to stop playing church and be the church. And to do that, there must be a shift in our mindsets.

Josh read this in his journal to me the other day. I thought it was so powerful, "The most valuable thing on this planet is a human soul, so much so that heaven and hell war over them daily." Now, I want you to ask yourself, "How much time do I spend going to war over the most valuable thing on the planet?"

At Clawson, one of our values is, "This church is a battleship, not a cruise ship." This is what this series is going to be all about. And if you are taking notes, this morning, the title of the series is "The Battleship Church" (Canon detonates).

We built the top of a battleship on the stage. Directly after the intro, we shot two explosions through the cannons

Josh Poage:

I want to start a little bit differently than I usually do. I want to read you what I wrote in my journal on September 21.

But before I read it, I want to share with you what has been going on in my spirit and what has built up to this point. Several months ago, God began putting in my spirit "Wake up,

Sleeper." It is time for the church of Jesus to wake up and be empowered to be the church he has called us to be. I said over and over again for about six months that "If the gates of hell are not going to prevail against the church," then the church is going to have to be empowered with the gifts of the Holy Spirit. Since then, many gifts have been poured out on our church family.

Then, this last miracle night, in my spirit, I felt like the phrase for the night was "It is time for War." God is waking up his church, empowering it, and calling it to war. That is what has been in my spirit lately. Now, I want to read my journal entry on 9/21/23 to you.

9/21/2023

The word that I believe the Lord is speaking to us for the season that we are in right now is "It is time for war." I think the word for the last season was, "Your next battle will be won in worship." And I believe that the worship at Clawson has been transformed dramatically over the previous 12 months. Battles and victories have occurred in our worship time and will continue to. But it is time for us to take the next step.

So, what does the phrase "It is time for war" mean? How does that affect the church family?

As I was praying today, the Lord spoke several things to me. I prayed with Pastors Brett Tessitore, Jeremy Cambell, Conner Harper, and our interns. As I prayed, I lay on the floor crying to God. And I heard the Lord say to me, "I want this... Josh, I want you to do this. I want you on your face to pray, pour out your heart, and listen to me as I lead. Would you please put prayer, power, and communion with me over fun and relevancy? Josh, it's time for war. I want you to rally the youth, I want you to muster the kids, I want you to rally the troops, and I want you to Storm the Gates of Hell in prayer. Attack the darkness; don't just defend against it.

During our prayer meeting, one of the guys said this. I just cannot get this out of my spirit, "The most valuable thing on this planet is a human soul, so much so that heaven and hell war over them daily. I want you to join that war." This whole last month (Fool's Gold) has been God showing us things that we thought to be valuable that were not. He wants us to refocus on what is valuable, and the most valuable thing we can be working on or fighting for is the human soul. That is what heaven and hell are wearing over day and night.

I believe in the season that we are moving into. It is a season of powerful supernatural prayer. It is going to be important for our staff to join that war. It is going to be important for our deacons to join that war. It is going to be important for our youth to join that war. It is going to be important for our kids to join that war. It's going to be essential for you to join the battle. God is saying it is time to rally everyone in prayer, storm the gates of hell, and push back the darkness!

Let me quickly give you the memory verse for this series of messages. You have the next five weeks to recite it at the gift shop. Then, I'm going to share with you what we will cover over the next five weeks, and then we will dive into the content for this morning.

Matthew 28:19-20 New Living Translation

"19 Therefore, go and make disciples of all the nations,[a] baptizing them in the name of the Father and the Son and the Holy Spirit. 20 Teach these new disciples to obey all the commands I have given you. And be sure of this: I am with you always, even to the end of the age."

I chose this scripture as the foundational scripture for this series because I want us to focus this month on the difference between being a believer in Jesus and a disciple of Jesus.

Let me give you our understanding of Disciple and Believer.

A disciple is a personal follower of Jesus during his life, a follower, student, or trainee of a teacher or leader.

On the other hand, a believer professes absolute belief in something.

Okay, the question is, is a Christian person a believer? It's not a tricky question. To be a Christian, you have to be a believer. Is the Devil, the demons, or his army believers? Yes.

James 2:19 New Living Translation

19 You say you have faith, for you believe that there is one God.[a] Good for you! Even the demons believe this, and they tremble in terror.

Is believing in God or Jesus going to get you to heaven? The correct answer to that question is no. Believing in Jesus in the English sense of the word will not get you to Heaven. Some of you may be thinking, 'Hold on, Pastor, in Romans, that's what it says.' So, let's look at that.

Romans 10:9-10 New Living Translation

"9 If you openly declare that Jesus is Lord and believe in your heart that God raised him from the dead, you will be saved. 10 For it is by believing in your heart that you are made right with God, and it is by openly declaring your faith that you are saved."

If you are not careful, you can take the scripture out of context as you read this scripture. You could think that if you believe Jesus Christ is the son of God and confess with your mouth that he is the son of God, you are now saved. But the only people who believe that do not understand what the word "believe" means. There is an action piece that goes with this scripture after believing and confessing. It said, "It is by openly declaring your faith that you are saved."

The word "pisteuo" is a Greek word. Pisteuo means to have faith in, to entrust (especially one's spiritual well-being to Christ): -- believe(-r), put in trust with.

This word doesn't simply mean acknowledging that Jesus Christ is Lord and King; the devil acknowledges that. It is an action word that is saying because I have faith in Jesus Christ as my Lord and Savior, and I believe in Him. I am entrusting Him with my life and my spiritual well-being. That is so much different from what so many people believe today.

Jesus didn't come and die to build a body of believers simply to acknowledge that He is the savior but to do nothing more with that information. Jesus came to build an army of soldiers who, because they believe He is their savior, give up their life to follow Him and become a disciples. In the Greek definition of the word, that is what a believer is.

At Clawson, one of our values is "this church is a battleship, not a cruise ship." We believe God has called us to create disciples, mature followers, and soldiers to wage war against the enemy! We do not simply attract members to attend church. I believe that the church of America is in the state it is because too many pastors and churches have stopped training, stretching, and pushing people. Instead, we have started pampering them.

Let me ask you a question. What do you think would happen if our military took on this same approach? Instead of whipping the guys into shape and getting them ready for war, we just pampered them and made them feel good about themselves. Let's do our best not to make them uncomfortable. What would happen to those soldiers when they went into battle? They would get their butts kicked. Can I be vulnerable with you this morning? This is what is happening to the church. We have stopped training disciples, and we have been pampering members. When our members are stepping out into battle every single day, they are getting their butts kicked.

I heard that the most remarkable example of what is going on in the church right now is the 2023 Gateway Conference.

Have you ever heard the idiom an apple a day keeps the doctor away? Do you know why that is true? Apples have all kinds of nutrients and good stuff for your body. I wish that phrase was like a bag of grapes a day or some strawberries a day keeps the doctor away. I'm not a big apple kind of guy. But you know what kind of apples I like? I like some Carmel apples. I never want to eat an apple unless you put some caramel and some nuts on it, then I like some apples. Do you know what I learned this weekend? When you dip that apple in caramel and make it unforgettable, it completely cancels out the nutrients, and what was supposed to be a good thing for your body now won't do you any good at all. The candy cancels out the good.

What is happening in our culture is that the word of God is full of all these good things for our lives. But people don't love it the way it is, so we are seeing more and more pastors and leaders dipping the word of God into the culture to make the bible taste better. However, because it has been immersed in our culture, it cancels out the truth. It provides no transformation as we can't get to the nutrients through the culture.

The title for this series is "The Battleship Church," and the five things that we are going to be looking at over the next five weeks are; "Defining the Fight," I want you to leave this morning understanding the fight that is going on for every person's soul. Next week is "Defending Against the Enemy," then "The Fight for Souls," "Storming the Gates of Hell," and ending the series with a message entitled "Fight till Death."

To understand the fight that we are in, we need to know where this war came from. The very first battle of this war, which is still taking place, was in Heaven. Satan was created to be something great. It was believed that he led the angels in worship of God. He was beautiful — one of the top dogs in Heaven. But Satan's pride got the best of him, and he rose with an army of ⅓ of the angels and turned against God. It wasn't enough for him to serve God; he wanted to be God. God then cast Satan out of heaven and down to earth. Then we see battle after battle. Satan with Eve, Satan with Job, Satan deceiving

God's children the same way he did with the angels in heaven. This war is going on because of everything that God has, Satan wants to take from Him.

So, then Jesus came to the earth to die so we could be saved. We see Satan try to turn Jesus against the father in Matthew 4, tempting him to turn to him. We know another battle when Jesus dies and is laid in the tomb. The bible says that Jesus took the struggle down to hell, and he put a whooping on Satan in Hell and took back the keys to death and the grave. But y'all, it is not over.

The truth is the war is still going on. Battle after battle is a war for our souls that will continue until the final judgment when God creates a new heaven and new earth. So, that is the war that I am going to be talking about for the next five weeks: the war between God and Satan, the war over people, the war for my soul and yours. Thinking about defining this war, I have three things that I would like to highlight and talk to you about today.

The Challenge of Recognizing the Fight

I think a huge problem is recognizing the fights we are having while they are going on. I believe the Lord has been speaking to me about shifting our mindset from a civilian to a soldier's mindset. A civilian and a soldier have different mindsets.

A civilian is not focused on war; we are not focused on defending ourselves or our families against the enemy. Our country's soldiers do that for us; because of that, war is the last thing on our minds. We are considering making money, new cars, clothes, and things, moving up in the world. We are not thinking about fighting in a war. That is a civilian mindset.

A soldier, on the other hand, is trained for battle. They wake, eat, move, and breathe war. Their mind is always on battle; even when they're not in a battle, they think about it. It should be the same way with the disciples of Jesus. We see this mindset with His first disciples.

We should be training for battle, maturing as soldiers, and learning how to fight. Instead, what we see in the church world are civilians who have joined the army yet have no idea how to fight. As a matter of fact, most of us don't even recognize when we are in a fight.

Have you ever heard people say things like I am just having a bad day today? Could it be that they are having a bad day because they are not recognizing that they are in a fight?

Has anyone ever seen the cartoons where you have the little angel and the little devil on your shoulders? The angel is trying to convince you to do right, but the devil is trying to persuade you to do wrong. Does anyone ever feel like that is a reality in your life? Something is whispering to you to do right, but at the same time, something is whispering for you to do wrong. Could it be that this is happening because we are in a war? The answer is yes, we are. Paul talks about this in Romans.

Romans 7:18-20 New Living Translation

"18 And I know that nothing good lives in me, that is, in my sinful nature.[a] I want to do what is right, but I can't. 19 I want to do what is good, but I don't. I don't want to do what is wrong, but I do it anyway. 20 But if I do what I don't want to do, I am not really the one doing wrong; it is sin living in me that does it."

Obviously, there is a war that is going on in Paul's mind.

Just because the battle is unseen, it doesn't mean it doesn't exist. Unseen does not equal unreal.

This inner war is going on for our souls, and we need to understand that it's affecting everything about our lives. We are often just going through life, not even recognizing the spiritual battles we are facing. I have learned that if you aren't ready for a fight, you will probably lose the fight. We have to learn to recognize the battles we are facing and learn how to fight.

The Battles We Face

A war consists of multiple battles. Did you know in the Civil War, hundreds, if not thousands, of battles made up that war? Some small battles took place, and some significant battles took place. Fifty major battles took place. Guess what? The South won some of those battles, and the North defeated others. Yet, only one side won the war.

I cannot tell you how many spiritual battles I have had, but I can tell you this: It is in the thousands. Battles of my faith, in my home, battles with addiction, religion, my marriage, kids, over people, battles in the church, and most of all, battles in my mind. I also want you to know that I have lost a lot of battles.

As a matter of fact, there was a time in my life when I thought I was going to lose the battle for my soul, and I didn't feel like it was worth fighting for anymore.

If you are here today and in the midst of a battle like that, or if you are struggling over this feeling like this is not worth fighting for anymore, let me give you just a little encouragement.

What I have found to be 100% true when it comes to us fighting battles with our spiritual enemy is this. If we try to fight our battles without God, we will lose the battles every time. Satan is more powerful than Josh, and he is more powerful than you are. But God, so far, has won every single battle that Satan has fought with him. In our lives, if we allow God to fight the battle, then it is a battle that Satan cannot win! God is more powerful than him.

I want you to know it doesn't matter what your last battle was, if you won it, or if you got beaten down. The only thing that matters is allowing God to be your strength. You get back up and will enable him to begin to fight through you on your behalf. Here is what you need to know: this is a battle you can win.

Don't you dare stop fighting because you lost a battle? Jesus wins the war in the end, and he will win the war over your soul if you will allow him to fight! He will win the battles that you face if you allow him to fight your battles through you.

So, we have looked at the challenges we sometimes have in recognizing the fight, war, and battles. We have talked about the battles we are facing. Now, I want you to consider this question in your mind.

Why Would I Want to Get Involved in a War?

How many of you would say, in most situations, your natural reaction is to fight? You have no problem with a fight. How many of you guys enjoy dealing with controversy?

How many of you would say your natural reaction is to stay out of everything? When someone attacks you or comes at you or your beliefs, your natural response is to remain neutral. You just try to calm everyone down. You don't want to fight, and you want peace with everybody. Here is what you need to understand: when it comes to the spiritual war that we are in, there is no Switzerland in spiritual warfare.

We don't get to be spiritual hippies. World peace is never going to happen. God and Satan are never going to get along. And to quote Black Hawk Down, "The decision you make now will affect the rest of your life."

If you choose not to fight in this war, you are choosing to fight for the enemy, which is what he wants you to do.

Church family, it is time for the Church of Jesus to stop getting beaten down! It is time for us to stop being lazy Christians! It is time for us to stop viewing and treating the church as a place to go and get fed so we can make it through the week!

It is time for the church of Jesus to step up and start training! It is time for church leaders to start leading! It is time for us to stop being believers and begin being disciples! It is time for us to learn how to fight, to be empowered by the Holy Spirit, and to stop getting beaten down by the enemy! Let's take the fight to them!

That is what this series is going to be about. We are training for war, and we are going to war.

We are becoming the battleship church that God called His church to be, and today, I am asking you to join me.

We are going to learn this month how to defend ourselves and our families, we are going to learn how to go after souls, and we are going to learn how to aggressively storm the gates of hell in prayer and spiritual warfare.

Response

If you are here right now and you feel like God is stirring up in you a passion for doing more, a desire to do more than just sit in a chair, and you feel like God is pushing you to step up and join the army, take back our families, our communities, our nation for Jesus and you are willing to fight and be devoted to that because I want you right now to take your phone out and text me this word, "Drafted."

It is time! It is time for the church to step up and be the church again! If you text me, just know I will be asking more from you because, as your pastor and captain, I will be training you to fight and win. So, if you are not serious, then don't text me.

If you would like to watch this message, please scan the QR Code below or visit Clawson.tv/battleship-church-one

Results

At the end of this message, from the 700 people who attended our weekend services, we had 133 people who texted me "drafted" to join the Army of Christ on the first day. People continued to participate throughout the week, and by Sunday, we had 163. I felt like the Holy Spirit led me to draft a bootcamp, even though, at that moment, I had no idea what I would be doing with them.

About two hours after I finished sharing that message with the church family on Sunday, I felt the Holy Spirit say to me, "I want you to take this army through boot camp and prepare them for battle." The next day was the start of the boot camp training.

Day 1

Morning recruits, BOOT CAMP STARTS NOW! I know it is early; rise and shine. Taking this seriously will change your life for the next 30 days. This week is all about shifting from the civilian mindset to a soldier.

Read

1 Peter 5:8 (I want you to know what the enemy is doing right now.)

Matthew 4 (This is where Satan is tempting Jesus)

Today, I want you to begin to recognize your battles. Then, write them down when you see the attacks. I would love for you to text me as you see the enemy's work. Before you do anything else this morning, pray to the Father to open your spiritual eyes to the war around you. As your captain, I am here for whatever you need. I got your six soldiers. Praying for you this morning.

- Captain Joshua

Journal

_____

_____

_____

_____

_____

_____

_____

_____

_____

_____

_____

_____

_____

_____

_____

_____

_____

_____

_____

_____

_____

_____

Day 2

Good morning, Soldier. I hope you are ready for Day 2 of BOOT CAMP! It is 6 am, and it is time to get up and work out. Knowing the enemy and his goal is essential when getting ready for war!

What does the devil do?

He steals God's word from you.
He sets traps to ensnare you.
He fights to stop you.
He plans to destroy you.

Think back to the war going on yesterday around you.

Where did you see the enemy attack?
Where did you lose the battle?
Where did you see victory?

Write a journal about yesterday's attacks, why you were defeated, or how you could win.

Listen

"I'm Listening" by Chris McClarney.

Listen for God to speak to you.

Read

Ephesians 6:10-18

This is what I am going to be preaching about this weekend. Which ones do you need to put in place to defeat the enemy? I got your six. Let me know if you need me! Heavenly Father gives us spiritual insight and discernment to see and understand what the enemy is doing around us.

- Captain Joshua

Journal

Day 3

Morning Soldier! Day 3 of BOOT CAMP starts now. Man, what a morning! I woke up this morning, and my phone won't work. Attack number 1 for the day. The enemy is trying to stop this text from going out. This week is all about recognizing the fight around you. Today, I want you to identify the people that the enemy uses to come at you, attack you, tempt you, and cause you to fail.

If you show me your friends, I'll show you a picture of your future. Who are you leaning on, who are your friends, who are you allowing to influence your life? Is it possible that the enemy is using them to attack you, and you may not even know it?

Listen

"Battle Belongs"

Today, I want you to recognize the battles you are facing. Who they are coming from and allow God to fight the battle. At the end of the day, journal who the enemy used to attack, tempt, or come at you and how you responded.

This week is all about shifting the mindset from civilian to soldier. If you can begin to recognize who Satan is using to attack you, you can be more ready for it in the future. You got this! I got your back! It's going to be a great day. Let me know if you need me, and I would love to hear how God is shifting your mindset and showing you the war around you. Before you leave your house, pray God will open your eyes to see the war around you. Have a great day, soldier - Captain Joshua.

Journal

_____
_____
_____
_____
_____
_____
_____
_____
_____
_____
_____
_____
_____
_____
_____
_____
_____
_____
_____
_____
_____
_____
_____

Day 4

Morning soldier! Day 4 is here, so get up. It is time for training. The war around us is becoming more evident. Yesterday, I recognized various ways the enemy used people, and God used people to influence. Our eyes must be opened to realize that work.

Today, your focus and training are all about recognizing the enemy's work at certain places and the creation of God. Sometimes, in church, you see the work of both. Today, I want you to focus on areas where you know the work and influence of the enemy and the work of God.

Right now, before you leave that house:

Listen

"Fear is not my future by Maverick City."

Ask God to speak to you this morning through the word.

Read

2 Timothy 2:8-10

Journal what you sense the Lord is telling you. Pray for your eyes to continue to be open. Pray for your growth, marriage, family, and church. It is going to be a great day, Soldier. I got your back if you need me. I would love to hear all about what God is doing in you and showing you. - Captain Joshua

Journal

Day 5

Morning soldier! Day 5, and it is time to get up and begin training. I know you're tired. I know you are worn out. The war is always going on, and we must always be ready for what is coming.

I hope that your training is going well. At this point, you should recognize people the enemy uses to attack you. You should recognize places the enemy uses to attack or influence you. As you go throughout your day today, I want you to start recognizing things in your life that bring on attacks, make you struggle, or that the enemy uses. For example, a cell phone and a computer are two things that the enemy uses in a huge way to tempt us.

Get up!

Listen

"See a Victory" by Elevation Worship

Read

James 1:2-18

Journal what the lord speaks to you in your training time. As you see things that Satan is using to attack you or tempt you, journal about them, too. I know this is a lot of work, but if you take this seriously, you are shifting your mindset from the natural to the spiritual. And use discernment to see the work of the enemy and the work of God. Good Luck, soldier, you got this. I am here for anything that you might need. NOW, GET TO WORK - Captain Joshua.

Journal

Day 6

Morning Soldier! Today is Day 6, and I know you probably thought today was your day off from '6 am wake-up and workout' because it is Saturday. Satan's Army is not sleeping in, so neither are we.

Today is the last day that our focus is entirely on switching our mindset from 'Civilian or Earthly' to 'Soldier or Heavenly.' From now on, that is a must. Today, I want you to spend the whole day recognising the spiritual battles, no matter where you are. The people, places, and things around you are where God and the enemy work. Write down your thoughts, and as you recognize the battles, pray.

Listen

"Egypt" by Bethel Music.

Read

James 1:19-27

I was hoping you could practice what these scriptures tell us to do today, especially verse 19. Then, write down what you feel God is speaking specifically to you and where he is challenging and stretching you. It has been a great first week. I can't wait to see you guys tonight at 6 pm or tomorrow at 10:30 am. If you need me, just radio for some support - Captain Joshua.

Journal

Day 7

Good morning, Soldier. This is day 7 of your Boot Camp training. After today, you are one week down and a lifetime of warfare to go. I believe that God will do some work for you. From here on out, the goal is that you will have the discernment to see the work of God and the work of the enemy as it happens around you.

Today, we are moving our focus onto some other training. The message this weekend is "From Bootcamp to Battlefield". It is all about getting in shape, learning your weapons and how to use them and getting filled with and empowered by the Holy Spirit.

Listen

"Rest on Us" by Maverick City

If you are not filled with the baptism of the Holy Spirit in your quiet time while listening to this song, ask God to fill you with His holy spirit and power so that you can be ready for war. Ask your captain if you have any questions about the holy spirit or baptism of the holy spirit. We have continued to have people join us throughout the week! We now have 163 people drafted into this army right now. My prayer is through this boot camp, God will empower you. You will begin using the unique abilities He has given you. Get ready because your life is about to change.

Write about what happened in your quiet time this morning, and write what you believe God is speaking to you - Captain Joshua.

Journal

Week 2

"Bootcamp 101 - From Bootcamp to Battlefield"

Good day, Clawson family! I have to ask: for those of you who decided to respond to the message last week and got drafted into the army, how many of you would say that it has been a challenging week? How many of you would say, more than ever, that God is beginning to open your eyes to the warfare that is going on around you?

For those who were not here or did not get drafted, we kicked off this series, "The Battleship Church," last week. The message was about recognizing the fight we are in — learning to see the spiritual war around us. In response to the message, I said if you would like to be trained in the army of Christ to begin to wage war against the darkness, would you text me the word 'drafted'? And check this out: Between our two-weekend services, we had 163 people drafted into the army.

So, this week, those 163 people started boot camp. And Just like boot camp, I woke them up early in the morning. They had to do some spiritual training, and this week was all about switching our mindsets from civilian to soldier. They have been praying every single day for God to open their spiritual eyes to see the battles that are going on around them, and God is beginning to do that in their lives. This week, I have heard tons of testimonies about what God has been doing to these soldiers.

If you were not here and would like to be drafted into this boot camp, I can catch you up this week, but you will be doing double the work. If you want to start the spiritual boot camp, would you text me the word 'drafted,' and I will get you started this week?

Our memory verse for this particular series is:

Matthew 28:19-20 New Living Translation

"19 Therefore, go and make disciples of all the nations,[a] baptizing them in the name of the Father and the Son and the Holy Spirit. 20 Teach these new disciples to obey all the commands I have given you. And be sure of this: I am with you always, even to the end of the age."

You can recite your memory verses at the gift shop in the back. It is the first year of doing memory verses. We have had a lot of fun with it and given away several cool stuff. At the end of the year, you could win a cruise if your name gets drawn from those doing their memory verses. For more info on that, go to the gift shop.

Again, I want to share that this scripture is the foundational verse for this series because I want us to understand that there is a difference between being a *believer* in Christ and a *disciple* of Christ. God wants more from us than to acknowledge that he is our saviour. He wants us to follow Him and His path for our lives. He wants us to develop into soldiers for His kingdom. Disciples, which is our goal here at Clawson, is creating *disciples*.

So, if you are taking notes today, the message's title is "From Bootcamp to Battlefield."

Let me share with you how this message came about because I initially did not plan on preaching this topic. I spent most of Monday and Tuesday writing the message, "Defending against the enemy," because that is what I was going to speak on. Wednesday morning, I was meeting with Dr. Paul and Mrs. Tanya Potter. The meeting was to get his thoughts on training for boot camp. As he talks, he suddenly says something about being filled with the holy spirit and empowered to fight the battles. Everything in me froze up. The Lord told me, "Before you can ever defend against the enemy, you have to know how to use the weapons for the war."

Today will be about learning your weapons and how to use them. When you go to boot camp, they inform you about the types of battles that you will be facing, which is what we did last week, and then they equip you to confront them. They teach you how to use your weapons. You can't defend against the enemy if you haven't been through the boot camp. So, today is all about learning your weapons, and I will take you from boot camp to the battlefield.

There are several things you have to focus on in boot camp, but the very first thing you have to do is:

Get in Shape to Fight

First, they mentally and emotionally get you into shape.

They completely strip you of the identity you have. You have to get the same haircut. We all got to wear the same clothes and shoes, sleep on the same beds, and use the same showers. The military owns you; the sooner you get that in your head, the better soldier you will be. It takes me back to last week when I talked about shifting from a civilian mindset to a soldier mindset and makes me think of the scripture:

1 Corinthians 6:19-20 New Living Translation

"19 Don't you realize that your body is the temple of the Holy Spirit, who lives in you and was given to you by God? You do not belong to yourself, 20 for God bought you with a high price. So, you must honor God with your body."

In spiritual boot camp, we must do the same: get ourselves mentally in shape. For those of you taking this drafting into the army thing seriously, this whole week has been about bringing you mentally in shape. The sooner we understand that we no longer belong to ourselves, the sooner we can switch our minds from civilian to soldier, and the better soldier for Christ we can become.

Next, in boot camp, they start working on that physical shape. You have to be in good physical condition to be a soldier. You must be strong, get up at the crack of dawn to run and work out, shoot, work together with your unit, know how to fight and have self-control.

To learn to walk in unison, take orders, fold your clothes right, receive discipline and correction, and learn to do all the things you must do, you must master self-control. You will not make it in the military if you cannot do that.

Now, I want you to hear me. It is precisely the same way in the spiritual war we are facing.

1 Timothy 4:8 NLT

"8 Physical training is good, but training for godliness is much better, promising benefits in this life and in the life to come."

Physically, we have to train for godliness; part of that is mastering self-control. Sometimes, we blame satan for doing things we did, and then we blame him because it makes us feel better to think he did it. We give satan a lot more credit than he deserves. Everything in your life is not demons coming at you. Sometimes life sucks, and sometimes my actions bring about consequences that have nothing to do with satan; they have to do with me.

Listen, satan did not open your mouth and make you say those things you shouldn't have said, and you did that. Satan didn't make you eat the entire dozen doughnuts; you did that. Satan did not make you type the porn site on your computer; you did that. And for you to learn how to be a soldier for the kingdom of heaven, you will not only have to deal with the enemy of the kingdom of darkness. You will have to deal with the enemy of your flesh, and the only way to do that is self-discipline.

2 Timothy 1:7 New Living Translation

"7 For God has not given us a spirit of fear and timidity, but of power, love, and self-discipline."

You must discipline yourself to be the warrior Jesus wants you to be. Destroy your flesh, shift your mind, let go of the sins you have held onto, stop making excuses, put up walls of protection, and get accountability. All of these things must happen for you to learn self-discipline. But just like in the military, when you learn to be disciplined and you learn your enemy, you can be a very effective soldier. In the army of Jesus, to be effective, you must be disciplined and know who your enemy is.

So, you have got to get in shape mentally, emotionally, and physically, and to fight in the spiritual war, you have got to get in shape spiritually. This moves me to the next point. To go from the boot camp to the battlefield, you have to:

Understand Your Weapons

In the military, the primary weapon you use is a gun, and you have to know everything about this gun. You have to know how to load the gun, shoot it, clean it, take it apart if it gets jammed, and fix it while in the middle of the fighting. This gun is the weapon you use; before you ever go into the field, you must be able to use it flawlessly.

Once you get good at it, you learn to use other weapons: handguns, grenades, assault rifles, grenade launchers, sniper rifles, RPGs, tanks, etc. You have to learn how to use all sorts of cool weapons if you are going to use them in the field.

When it comes to training in the spiritual army, you must do the same thing. God has given us a ton of cool weapons, and if you can learn to use them effectively and know when and how to use them, you will be effective in the fight.

The three most basic weapons for a soldier of Christ are worship, the word of God, and prayer. So, let's talk briefly about how to use these weapons.

How many of you guys love to worship the Lord? If you don't believe that worship can be used as a weapon, I want you to know there are many examples of this in the Bible, and '2 Chronicles 20' would be one of them.

2 Chronicles 20:22 New Living Translation

"22 At the very moment they began to sing and give praise, the LORD caused the armies of Ammon, Moab, and Mount Seir to start fighting among themselves."

They worshipped God, and God fought the battle they were facing. Jesus tells us that even the rocks will cry out if we do not worship. Worship pleases God. So, we see and find in scripture that when his people worship Him, and He is pleased with them, He literally steps in to fight with and for them.

Sometimes, we see this in the physical, like in this case, where God steps in and fights their physical battle. But sometimes, that is just in the spiritual.

For example, how many of you have ever had a spiritual battle won during worship? Depression left you, and addiction broke off of you. You received healing, filled with the spirit, or some other kind of battle. To be honest with you, when my battle is in my mind, I find worship to be the most effective weapon because God uses the praise that I give him to strengthen me and fight with me. Use your worship as a weapon. It's not just a good song to sing.

The second weapon is your word; let me give you a couple of scriptures on the word.

Ephesians 6:17 New Living Translation

"17 Put on salvation as your helmet, and take the sword of the Spirit, which is the word of God."

Hebrews 4:12 New Living Translation

"12 For the word of God is alive and powerful. It is sharper than the sharpest two-edged sword, cutting between soul and spirit, between joint and marrow. It exposes our innermost thoughts and desires."

During this portion, we brought out a double-edged sword as a reference

This is the weapon that Jesus used on satan when satan came to tempt him in Matthew 4. Every time satan attacked, Jesus shot back at him with the word, with truth. Most Christians don't know how to use the word of God, mainly because they don't know the word of God. Just like if I don't remember my gun in physical warfare, I will have a problem. Similarly, if we don't know our word in spiritual warfare, we will have a problem.

When you begin to see and understand the battles, you will find that most of the time, satan attacks with deception, he attacks with lies, and he attacks with little twists of the truth. That is why if you know the truth, you can laugh at him and fire right back at him with the truth. If you don't know the truth, you can't use it to attack, and you will often be deceived into believing that his lie is true.

Let's have a couple of examples. Satan begins to attack me with fear. How do I strike back?

No, not fear. God has not given us the spirit of fear but of power, love, and a sound mind.

What about If satan attacks my identity?

I have been adopted into the family of God, is what Paul says. Satan is just pissed because God isn't his family.

I brought out my AR-15for dramatic effect.

If you know the word, you can load your magazine with 66 boxes of ammo, and when satan comes knocking, you can lift your weapon and say, "Say hello to my little friend." But you have to know the word and what it means to use it to attack back.

So, we have the weapon of worship and the weapon of the word. On number three, I will do a whole message in three weeks called "Storm the Gates of Hell." So, I will not stay here long, but the 3rd weapon is;

Prayer

James 5:16 New Living Translation

16 *"Confess your sins to each other and pray for each other so that you may be healed. The earnest prayer of a righteous person has great power and produces wonderful results."*

Matthew 18:18-20 New King James Version

18 "Assuredly, I say to you, whatever you bind on earth will be bound in heaven, and whatever you loose on earth will be loosed in heaven.19 "Again[a] I say to you that if two of you agree on earth concerning anything that they ask, it will be done for them by My Father in heaven. 20 For where two or three are gathered together in My name, I am there in the midst of them."

We aggressively pushed back the darkness in our 9:00 prayer meeting this morning. We are training and learning how to pray for people or situations and together in unity to see where the enemy is at work and fire everything we have at him.

Jesus gave us his authority, and when we got to the Father, led by the holy spirit, with the authority of Jesus Christ, there is power in our prayer life. There is power when we command the enemy to leave; when we attack evil spirits, the bible says we can tear down strongholds. You need to be here in three weeks when we discuss this.

So, as we go through basic training and boot camp, the first three weapons we must learn to use against the enemy's attacks are worship, the word of God, and prayer.

In the military, though, there is not just basic training. Once you learn to use your primary weapons, those who want to be even more effective in warfare can be on special forces teams. The Green Berets, Night Stalkers, Rangers, Seals, Marine Raiders, Force Recon, tactical air, and paratroopers. These people specialize in specific styles of warfare.

Now, you may not know this, but in the Army of Christ, there are special teams also. This is the 3rd thing I want to talk to you about today.

Special Forces

I want to show you some cool things Jesus gave his army. First of all, he gave us special officers.

Ephesians 4:11-12 New Living Translation

11 "Now these are the gifts Christ gave to the church: the apostles, the prophets, the evangelists, and the pastors and teachers. 12 Their responsibility is to equip God's people to do his work and build up the church, the body of Christ."

I was talking to a couple of pastor buddies I pray with on Thursdays this week, and it was pretty funny. All of us are pastoring in some form or fashion. We all know God has placed us where we are, but none of us are gifted to pastor. We had an apostle, an evangelist, and a prophet in the room.

I told them I believe we have seen in the church world that pastors try to hold all five of these offices. The five-fold ministry is not equipping church people because they are trying to work in offices that are not their own.

I am honored to lead this church and be your pastor, and I don't ever plan on changing that, but my giftings and office that God has equipped me in are that of an apostle, and I am beginning to work outside of Clawson in that, too.

Training, appointing, and equipping the church for the work of the kingdom. We have tons of pastors in this church. Paul Nolan is a shepherd, Christian Womack is a shepherd, and Josh Richards is a shepherd. We have two to three prophets working in the church right now and others training in that. My dad (Kevin Poage), Josiah Patterson, and Sheila Whitaker are all fantastic teachers, including about fifteen more teachers. We have Justin Puzz, Chris Morrison, Nick Guse, and Susie Wilkinson, who are evangelists.

Watch this: when all of these people understand their office and their role and come together for the equipping of the saints, you begin to see all of the five-fold ministry come about. If God is calling you for ministry, you need to understand what role he wants you to work in. So, those are the officers in the army of Christ.

Now, I am getting to my favorite part of this message. Jesus didn't just give us basic training, basic weapons, and officers to equip us.

He sent his holy spirit to empower us with supernatural powers to join the special forces teams.

In Luke 24:49, Jesus told the disciples, "I am sending you the Holy Spirit, who will fill you with Power from Heaven." So, God gives us special abilities and superpowers to be on his special forces teams. I want to show you this in scripture.

1 Corinthians 12:1, 7-11 New Living Translation

"1 Now, dear brothers and sisters,[a] regarding your question about the special abilities the Spirit gives us. I don't want you to misunderstand this."

"7 A spiritual gift is given to each of us so we can help each other. 8 To one person, the Spirit gives the ability to give wise advice[b]; to another, the same Spirit gives a message of special knowledge.[c] 9 The same Spirit gives great faith to another, and to someone else, the one Spirit gives the gift of healing. 10 He gives one person the power to perform miracles and another the ability to prophesy. He gives someone else the ability to discern whether a message is from the

Spirit of God or from another spirit. Still, another person is given the ability to speak in unknown languages, [d] while another is given the ability to interpret what is being said. 11 It is the one and only Spirit who distributes all these gifts. He alone decides which gift each person should have."

Listen to me: The Holy Spirit gives out gifts to us for us to be the most effective we can be for his army, and I want you to check this out. 87% of Christians say that they don't know what their spiritual gift is! That means nine out of ten Christians are about 500 in the worship center right now. That means 450 out of 500 of us are not working on our gifts because we don't know what they are.

If you are sitting here this morning and saying, "Hey, Pastor, that's me! How do I discover my gifts? Let me give you five quick thoughts, and then I will close this up."

1. Study what the Bible says about the gifts. Look at it, study it. 1 Corinthians 12, Romans 12, Ephesians 4 (talks about the 5-fold gifts of the ministry), and 1 Peter 4; read those chapters and study them.

2. Ask God to show you your gifts. "God, what gifts have you given me?" Watch as he does, and when he starts to do it, ask him, "Where do you want me to use these gifts? How do you want me to use these to make a difference?"

3. Examine what you enjoy and do well. If you're gifted, you will enjoy using your gifts and do them well. If you say, "I never want to help anybody; I hate being called upon to help!" You probably don't have the gift of serving. Okay? You don't enjoy it, and you don't do it well. Ask yourself what do you want and what do you do well.

4. Take a spiritual gifts test. It isn't going to be foolproof, but there are tests online. We also offer one in the growth track class.

5. Most importantly, do what the Holy Spirit leads you to do. Whenever you feel like God is calling you to do something, have the faith to do it.

Here is the cool news about God's army! In the military, the special forces are only for the elite few and those with natural talents.

1 Corinthians 12:10 says the Holy Spirit is the one who gives out the gifts for all believers. God has unique abilities and superpowers that he wants to give you as you battle against the darkness, and that starts with being filled with the Holy Spirit.

Next week is the 'Fight for Souls,' then 'Defending Against the Enemy,' then 'Storming the Gates of Hell.' I promise you if you are serious about being in the army of God and being effective for his Kingdom, you do not want to miss one of these messages.

So, today was all about getting us battlefield-ready. Getting in shape to fight, learning and using our weapons of worship, the word and prayer, and receiving the baptism of the Holy Spirit to empower the spiritual abilities God gives us to fight with. ALTAR TEAM, would you join me?

For the sake of clarity, I would like to give some direction on getting filled with the baptism of the HS. It was so cool this week. I had two text messages of people getting filled with the baptism of the Holy Spirit while doing their boot camp stuff in the mornings. It is not complicated, and we have made it that way.

In the scriptures, there are five Acts where people are filled with the Holy Spirit. Acts Chapter 2, the first time it happened. All they were doing was praying. No one was touching people and telling them to speak a different language. No one had to coach them on what to do. God did it all by himself. Then, another time was when Peter was preaching. It must have been a heck of a message because, during the preaching, the Bible says people were filled with the spirit and began to speak in other tongues. Then, on another occasion, in Acts, it says they placed their hands on them, prayed, and received the Holy Spirit.

So, according to scripture, the Holy Spirit was given through prayer, preaching, and the laying on of hands. It means you don't have to come to the altar and "pray through" to get the

Holy Spirit. You can get filled at home, by yourself, while praying, in a group, during preaching. Don't be scared of Him; seek Him, and you will find Him. Ask Him to be filled, be patient, and continue to seek Him until you are filled, just like they did in the Bible.

Response

Our worship team is about to come and lead us in some warfare. If you are in battle and you want to go and use your weapon of worship in just a minute, I want to invite you to come to the front and do so.

If you are here and would like to be filled with the Holy Spirit and power of God today, I invite you to come.

If you need to join the army of Christ, you are away from the Lord and must get things right with Him.

If you need prayer for wisdom, guidance, or healing, come now.

Don't allow satan to stop you from getting what you need today.

If you would like to watch this message, please scan the QR Code below or visit Clawson.tv/battleship-church-two

Results from the Message

There was a great response to the message; several people were filled with the Holy Spirit and refilled with the Holy Spirit. We also had another 68 people text in "drafted," which moved our number of boot campers to 201 who were now going through the six weeks of boot camp.

The new 68 people had to do week one and week two of boot camp all in one week. Still, man, the excitement that is going on in the church right now as people are getting serious about being practical for Jesus is amazing.

Day 8

Good morning, soldier. It's day eight of boot camp and a brand-new start to the week. Training this week will be all about using the weapons that God has given us. If you have not been filled with and empowered by the Holy Spirit, then this week, we ask God every morning during training to fill and empower us with his Holy Spirit. If you are filled with the spirit, ask God to train you in the special abilities the Spirit gives.

Today, our focus is on the weapon of worship. Let's get your heart prepared for worship.

Read

Romans 12:1-2,
John 4:21-24
Psalms 150.

Listen

"Take you at your word" by Cody Carnes
"Waymaker" by Highpointe Worship

Let these songs remind you today of who your God is.

Today, with every battle you are facing, I want you to go back to these songs and remind yourself that God is the waymaker. You can trust his word. Instead of allowing Satan to win the battle in your mind, get close to God and watch God fight your battle for you. It's going to be a fantastic day. I am a call or text away if you need anything from me. Praying for you today - Captain Joshua.

Journal

_____

_____

_____

_____

_____

_____

_____

_____

_____

_____

_____

_____

_____

_____

_____

_____

_____

_____

_____

_____

_____

_____

_____

Day 9

     Good morning, soldier. It's day nine of boot camp. Get up and get ready for training. Last week was all about recognizing the fight around you, and I hope you are continuing to focus on that and get better at it. This week is all about learning to use your weapons. Today, we will practice with one of your most potent weapons, the word of God.

Read

2 Timothy 3:16-17
Hebrews 4:12
Psalms 119:9;105
James 1:22

     These scriptures describe the power of the word and the purpose of the word, which is to be the lamp unto our feet and light unto our path.

Listen

"God I look to you" by Bethel music.

Today, as satan attacks you, I want you to use the same weapon Jesus used with satan. Use these scriptures, and begin to research scriptures you know you will need in the future to fire at satan. Keep walking in victory, soldier; I got your six. If you need anything, give me a call. Praying for you!

- Captain Joshua

Journal

Day 10

Good morning, soldier. It's day ten of the boot camp. Today, our training is about the weapon prayer. I think this is a weapon that we take for granted. Sometimes, we pray because we have been told to, but I don't think we fully understand the power of prayer. If we did, we would pray differently and more.

Read

Philippians 4:6–7
James 5:16
Matthew 6:5-13

Listen

"Wait on You" by Elevation Worship.

I want you to begin to pray that God would equip you with great faith so that when you go to God, you will have faith in what you are praying for.

Today, I want you to attempt to pray in all things and listen to God as He is speaking to you. Pray as you get up. Pray that God would draw close to you as you are to Him. Pray for your church, family, and the people you work with. Get offensive, and as God is showing you the enemy's work, pray against those things.

Begin your training today in the weapon of prayer. I want to hear how it is going. I want to hear where you are struggling. I want to help you in any way that I can. You've got this; keep pushing, training, and going! You got an army of people fighting with you. Let's push back the darkness and give the kingdom of satan a black eye today. I got your back, soldier

- Captain Joshua.

Journal

Day 11

Good morning, soldier. It's day eleven of the boot camp. Today's training will be about when to use the weapons you are training with. You have started training using your worship, word, and prayer life. Just like in military training, a soldier must learn when to use his sidearm, rifle, and grenade. We must learn how and when to use our weapons in spiritual military training. Sometimes, we have so much war going on that we have to use all of them.

When I am discouraged, my greatest weapon to fight is worship. When I am tempted, or satan is trying to deceive me, it is the word. When I am attacking the forces of darkness, it is prayer.

Read

Galatians 5:16-26

Listen

"God Problems" by Maverick City

Your training today is to Listen to the Holy Spirit and use your weapons as you need them to defend against and attack the enemy. See you on the battlefield

- Captain Joshua.

Journal

Day 12

Good morning, soldier. It's day twelve of the boot camp, almost two weeks down. I hope God is helping you shift from civilian to soldier. I hope you are learning to use your weapons for protection and attack.

For today's training, we will be using everything you have learned so far, plus practicing listening to the voice of the Holy Spirit. At the same time, he leads you throughout the day.

Our mindset and weapons are ready, and we are listening for the Holy Spirit to guide us in battle.

Read

Romans 8

Listen

"Make Room" by Elyssa Smith and Community Music.

Journal what the Lord is speaking to you. Journal what He says to you and shows you throughout the day. It's going to be a great day, soldier. Now, get to training. Your life and the lives of those around you depend on it

-Captain Josh.

Journal

Day 13

Good morning, soldier. It's day 13 of the boot camp! It is time to get up and start training. If you are feeling and getting attacked this week, I want you to know you are not alone. We have declared war against powers of darkness, and they are unhappy about it. I want to encourage you today with this word. Do not quit the boot camp; do not step back in fear. Let this week ignite a fire in you to push harder! That is how a soldier makes it through basic training.

The past week, I talked about special ops training and being filled with the Holy Spirit and supernatural powers. I spoke of officers in the army of Christ (Apostles, Prophets, Evangelists, Pastors, and Teachers) and the nine gifts of the Holy Spirit.

Read

Acts 2:1-2
Acts 8:14-17
Acts 10:44-48

These are examples in the Bible of people being filled with the Holy Spirit and how it worked.

Listen

"House of Miracles" by Brandon Lake.
Spend some time alone with the Lord, praying for a deeper understanding of him, praying for clarification on your calling, and praying for you to be filled and empowered by the Holy Spirit.

Part of this week's boot camp is attending a pre-service prayer meeting. If you attend Saturday night, that prayer meeting is at 5 pm in the fellowship hall tonight. If you attend Sunday morning services, that prayer meeting is at 9 am Sunday in the Fellowship Hall. If you can make it, this is not an option. It is a command. It is part of training and will help prepare you for WAR. See you at training, soldiers

- Captain Josh.

Journal

Day 14

Good morning, soldier. It's day fourteen of the boot camp. Get up and get ready; the fight is on. There is a fight going on for our families, church, marriages, kids, and souls, and we can not afford to be tired. Now get up, and let's fight back.

Congratulations, today you will have completed the first two weeks of boot camp. This means up to this point; you have been trained to see the war that is going on around you, to spot the works of the enemy and the works of your allies. You should be learning how to use the weapons God has equipped you with. Now get ready because the training will only get more intense from here on out.

Today, you will learn you have a duty in "The Fight for Souls." It is not just the evangelist's job to reach people for Jesus and share the gospel. It is the job of every Christian.

Listen

"Send me out" by Fee.

Get this song in your spirit. I want you to pray for God to give you the heart to reach people, the words to say, and the boldness to do what he calls you to do. I will see you guys at 9 am for prayer in the fellowship hall,

- Captain Joshua.

Journal

Week 3

"The Fight for Souls"

What's up, Clawson family! I'm excited about everything God is doing in our church family. It is the third week of a six-week series we have put together called "The Battleship Church."

So far, we have talked about recognizing the war around us. Where the enemy is moving and where God is moving. We have talked about training to use the weapons that God has given us. The weapons of worship, prayer, and the word of God. We also spoke for just a few minutes about special ops training and developing and learning to use the special abilities that the Spirit gives when we are filled with the Holy Spirit. We talked for just a minute about the officers in the armies of the Lord: apostles, prophets, evangelists, pastors, and teachers.

How many of you went home this week and did your boot camp training and would say that because of last week's message and training, you have become more effective at using the weapons God has given you? That is fantastic.

Our memory verse for this particular series is:

Matthew 28:19-20 New Living Translation

"19 Therefore, go and make disciples of all the nations,[a] baptizing them in the name of the Father and the Son and the Holy Spirit. 20 Teach these new disciples to obey all the commands I have given you. And be sure of this: I am with you always, even to the end of the age."

Today, if you are taking notes, I would like to preach a message called "Fight for Souls." The quote that keeps going through my mind repeatedly is, "The most valuable thing on this planet is a human soul, so much so that heaven and hell war over them daily." In this message, we will go into depth about the fact that we should be fighting for them, too, and what it looks like to first for Souls in our lives.

If you have your Bibles, I invite you to turn with me to Matthew 13, and I would like to read the parable of the sower to you.

Matthew 13:3-9 New Living Translation

"Listen! A farmer went out to plant some seeds. 4 As he scattered them across his field, some seeds fell on a footpath, and the birds came and ate them. 5 Other seeds fell on shallow soil with underlying rock. The seeds sprouted quickly because the soil was shallow. 6 But the plants soon wilted under the hot sun, and since they didn't have deep roots, they died. 7 Other seeds fell among thorns that grew up and choked out the tender plants. 8 Still other seeds fell on fertile soil, and they produced a crop that was thirty, sixty, and even a hundred times as much as had been planted! 9 Anyone with ears to hear should listen and understand."

Every one of the planted seeds represents a person or a soul in this story. So, suppose we will fight for souls for the kingdom of heaven. In that case, I believe that keeping this parable in mind, there are things that we can do that can make our harvesting or soul-winning for Jesus more successful. The first thing that I would like to encourage you to do is:

Prepare the Soil for the Seed

The seed that I am speaking of is the Gospel of Jesus. Going back to the Parable that Jesus shared in Matthew 13, it said that some seeds fell on the footpath, some fell on rocky soil, some fell on thorny soil, and some fell on good soil. Even the good soil didn't produce one hundredfold, though it was thirty, sixty, and one hundredfold.

What if there was a way to ensure that the seeds you were planting were planted in fertile soil instead of just chunking seeds everywhere that you could and seeing what sprouted up? I believe with all of my heart that we can work on the soil before we plant the seed and make it to where the seed we are planting has a much greater chance of sprouting and being healthy.

Not all people are ready to receive the gospel of Jesus. Some people have stoney hearts, some have thorny hearts, and some are ready to hear and receive the message. Also, Just because someone is not ready to receive Jesus doesn't mean we can't work on them to get them ready before we plant the seed. We have to recognize that church people have hurt some people in the past. When they think of Jesus, they think about those who hurt them. Some people have never heard the gospel and are not ready the first time they hear someone preach to them to commit to giving their life to something they just heard about.

For example, when I was young, I got very hard with the Gospel, church, or God. I did not have good soil. My soil was rocky and thorny and would not take a seed. But a lady who was a children's church pastor walked up to me and told me she liked my lip ring. I told her I don't think you are supposed to say that. Can't you get in trouble or something? And she just laughed and said, "I can like your lip ring if I want." Then, she began working on my heart without preaching the gospel and showing me a different version of Jesus than I had seen. She never preached the gospel to me, but the day I got saved, I was there where she asked me to be. Because of that relationship and all the work she had done for me, my heart was in a good place to receive the gospel, so I accepted the seed when the gospel was preached. That was in 2005, and now I have been serving the Lord for eighteen years.

Here is what I am saying: If we are going to be effective in this fight for souls, instead of preaching Jesus, we should run around being Jesus. He shares his love and shows people a version of Jesus they want to be like. A Jesus that loves and allows them to be authentic. As we do that, we take shovels, machetes, and tillers and prepare the soil for the seed we want to plant. So, number 1: Prepare the soil.

Plant the Seed

Y'all, I want to give some honor and celebrate with someone who is killing it at getting the soil ready and planting seeds of the Gospel. Stephanie Sowell is killing it. Y'all give it up for my girl Stephanie.

Stephanie Sowell and Elisa Kennedy gave their testimonies.

Over the last nine months, Stephanie has been completely delivered and just walking in this happiness and authority. And what she has been doing is all of the people in her life who have been skeptical of Jesus or not interested in Jesus are seeing this new Stephanie walking in this happiness and peace and coming to her for the answer.

Y'all know what the answer is? His name is Jesus. When you learn how to walk in the freedom of the identity he has given you, people should ask what is going on with you and how you can get some of that. So, all these people who have had hearts full of thorns and stones were having tons of conversations with Stephanie where she is telling them what God is doing in her life, and every time they have a conversation, thorns are cut down, stones are pulled up preparing the soil for the seed of the gospel. Then, she offers them the same freedom, and they are ready to receive the gospel.

Elisa and Kimberly were Stephanie's best friends, living lifestyles entirely away from Christ. They recently gave their lives to Christ and had complete turnarounds. The seed was planted when the soil was ready.

The truth is, we do not have to run around letting everyone know that they are going to hell without Jesus. That is just a big turn-off and is not effective at all. Actually, on the contrary, what that does is make people's hearts even more complex towards the gospel of Jesus cause the last thing they want to be like is these idiots running around condemning everyone else like the Pharisees.

The way to draw people to Jesus and get them ready for the seed or Gospel of Jesus is to be the hands and feet of Jesus. Then, when they are ready, you plant the seed.

What is the seed exactly? It is the Gospel. The Gospel is that God created us. We disobeyed him and were separated from Him. He sent Jesus to die on the cross for our sins so that we can be reconnected back to God. He desires that we follow Him and live the life he has planned for us. Humanity receives everything that we need through the Gospel of Christ.

Not everyone is ready to give their entire life to Christ when you plant the seed and share the gospel with them. It is actually ok. You are asking them to make a lifelong decision to follow Jesus; they need to ensure this is what they want. Look at what Jesus said about the cost of Discipleship in the Gospel of Luke.

Luke 14:25-33 New Living Translation

25 A large crowd was following Jesus. He turned around and said to them, 26 "If you want to be my disciple, you must, by comparison, hate everyone else — your father and mother, wife and children, brothers and sisters — yes, even your own life. Otherwise, you cannot be my disciple. 27 And if you do not carry your own cross and follow me, you cannot be my disciple.

28 "But don't begin until you count the cost. For who would begin construction of a building without first calculating the cost to see if there is enough money to finish it? 29 Otherwise, you might complete only the foundation before running out of money, and then everyone would laugh at you. 30 They would say, 'There's the person who started that building and couldn't afford to finish it!'

31 "Or what king would go to war against another king without first sitting down with his counselors to discuss whether his army of 10,000 could defeat the 20,000 soldiers marching against him? 32 And if he can't, he will send a delegation to discuss terms of peace while the enemy is still far away. 33 So you cannot become my disciple without giving up everything you own.

I did not choose to follow Jesus the first, second, or third time I heard the gospel. I counted the cost until I was ready to give what it would cost.

So, to fight for souls effectively, you prepare the soil (their hearts), plant the seed (the gospel of Christ), and number three.

Water the Seed

We don't do a great job of this in the church world. We plant the seeds of the gospel, and if someone gets saved, we count them as a number and move on to the following number. The issue is that this seed that has been planted needs to be taken care of. Without water, the seeds that are planted could die.

So, when someone accepts the seed of Jesus Christ, if I care about their soul, my job is now to help them grow into who God has for them to be. My job is to help them mature in the faith. They need to develop character by learning what God expects from them as Christians. They need to understand what ministry God has for them, and they need to learn how to be an authentic

Christian. They need to learn how to be a leader. All of this takes time. It is watering, watering, and maturing.

I don't know if you have ever planted a Garden, but let me tell you, taking care of the plants is no joke. It is hard work. The sun wanted to dry them out, the bugs tried to eat them, and the varmint wanted to get to them. Over the last several years, my dad has planted gardens. I have not done the work, but I watched him do it. The most I ever did was try to grow a pepper plant once. I learned I sucked at gardening because the bugs ate all my peppers.

My dad would be over there every single day. Pulling weeds, watering the plants, putting down fertilizer, and whatever needed to be done was what he was doing.

This should be the case in the church. When we plant seeds, we cannot just expect those seeds to turn into fruitful trees. We have to take care of them because satan is trying to kill that seed. The world is trying to take the focus. All hell is coming against the seeds we have planted, so we need to do whatever needs to be done to ensure that the seeds are ready to be harvested when harvest time comes. Lastly;

When the Harvest is Ready, Bring in the Harvest

I will never forget last summer. My dad had spent all his time planting potatoes, corn, okra, and peas; I don't even remember what else. Harvesting time came, and he called. He said, "Josh, I have you a row of potatoes. I want you to come and harvest them." Dad did all of the work. He planted the potatoes, watered them, and watched them daily. Then, when the harvesting time came, he called each of his kids and told us to go and harvest a row of potatoes. It makes me think of what Paul wrote to the church of Corinth.

1 Corinthians 3:6-9 New Living Translation

6 I planted the seed in your hearts, and Apollos watered it, but it was God who made it grow. 7 It's not important who does the planting, or who does the watering. What's important is that God makes the seed grow. 8 The one who plants and the one who waters work together with the same purpose. And both will be rewarded for their own hard work.

Dad did all the work, and we got to reap the rewards of his hard work. You know what this means as far as fighting for souls. It means we should always be doing the work. We should constantly be tilling up new ground and getting it ready for the seeds of Jesus. When the time is right, we should always plant seeds of the Gospel of Christ in people's lives. We should constantly water seeds that we've grown or someone else planted. When the time is right, we should always harvest souls into the kingdom. Right now, Jesus is looking for soldiers, warriors, and laborers who will be working and fighting for souls. Jesus told the disciples:

Matthew 9:37-38 New Living Translation

"37 He said to his disciples, "The harvest is great, but the workers are few. 38 So pray to the Lord who is in charge of the harvest; ask him to send more workers into his fields."

I ask you to join me in the fields as we look at the ground of souls around us. Let's do the work. Let's help people prepare their hearts for the Gospel, plant seeds of the Gospel, water the planted seeds, and bring in the harvest. Will you join me in the fight for souls? The day of the harvest is when Christ returns for his bride. Let's help get as many people ready for that day as possible.

Will you stand with me today?

I am asking for the response to today's message to be for us to go out in the fields that God has placed us and prepare, plant, water, and harvest. Will you join me?

Results from the Message

The results from this message were that we had many people commit to being laborers in the fields.

Our people, at this point, are already talking about the Battleship Church. It was all over Facebook, and now they had the keys to effectively harvesting.

Preparing the soil, planting the seed, watering the seeds already planted, and harvesting. We heard many stories of people doing these things in the next couple of weeks.

Day 15

Good morning, soldier! I hope you are ready for day fifteen of the boot camp. This week will separate those who are serious from those who are not. This week, your training will force you out of your comfort zone. Pastor Josh Rivera said, "If the Gospel hasn't impacted you, don't expect it to change someone else." How accurate is the Gospel of Jesus to you?

Today, I want you to focus on what the Gospel has done in your life. What is the Gospel to you? Reflect on all the things God has done that you can brag about. How has he transformed you? I want you to journal some things that God has done for you.

Read

1 Thessalonians 1:5
Romans 1:8-17

Listen

"Ain't Nobody" by Cody Carnes.

If the Gospel has genuinely changed and transformed you, I want you to brag today to someone about what the Gospel of Jesus is to you. Brag about how powerful your God has been in your life. Allow the Holy Spirit to open a door to share your faith. Then, journal about how it goes. I would also love to hear about how this goes. Do not cower in fear; you are a part of the war for souls. Allow God to lead you in doing your part. Let me know if you need a backup

- Captain Joshua.

Journal

Day 16

Get up, soldier. We don't have time for sleep. It is day sixteen of the boot camp, and we have a lot of training to do. Some souls are in danger of eternity without Jesus if we do not do our jobs.

Today, I want you to focus on being aware of the people around you. You have been trained to identify where the enemy is at work and where God is at work. Now, I want you to begin patterning with God to work on people.

If you listen and allow him to, God will open a door or direct you to pray for people today who need prayer. It may be a family member, a coworker, someone who makes your coffee, or a server at a restaurant. Listen as God leads you today, and I want to challenge you to pray for three people as the Lord directs your spirit.

Read

1 Timothy 2:1-7
Acts 10:19-20

Listen

"The Blessing" by Elevation Worship

So, as you are getting yourself mentally prepared for your training today, I want you to journal what the Lord speaks to you in your reading time. Journal how the Lord uses you today. I CAN'T WAIT TO HEAR ABOUT IT

- Captain Josh.

Journal

_____

_____

_____

_____

_____

_____

_____

_____

_____

_____

_____

_____

_____

_____

_____

_____

_____

_____

_____

_____

Day 17

Get up, soldier. Sleep is overrated. It is time for day seventeen of the boot camp. The war is waging, and let me just say you guys are sticking it to the enemy. I am so proud of you! We are beginning to see the effectiveness of our unity as an army fighting back. I believe together, we are pushing back the darkness in the spiritual realm. I will tell you we are making the enemy angry.

You must protect your heart, mind, marriage, family, home, and church. We also need to be praying for protection over Israel. Keep your eyes peeled. If you are not ready for it, satan is going to be able to hit you where it hurts.

Read

1 Corinthians 1:18-31

Listen

"Don't you give up on me" by Brandon Lake.

Today, let's take some more ground and push forward. Let's boast about the Lord and what He is doing today. I want you to talk to someone or multiple someones who are not serving the Lord about all of the cool things God is currently doing in your life

- Captain Josh.

Journal

Day 18

Good morning, soldier. It is time for training. It's day eighteen, and we are almost halfway through the boot camp. I want to encourage you not to stop! Not to stop halfway through the training but to dedicate yourself to growing and maturing into the soldier God has for you to be.

As I was thinking about today's training, I kept thinking about Philip's story. This man needed understanding, and God led Philip right to the place to give him the wisdom he needed, and the guy got saved.

Today, I want you to focus on seeking someone who needs understanding. Someone who needs the truth of the life-changing Gospel of Jesus. When God leads you, I want you to share the gospel and what Jesus has done in your life. You will be open and bold and listen as the spirit leads. He will open a door for you to plant seeds and change someone's life today.

Read

Acts 8:26-39

Listen

"Move Your Heart" by Maverick City.

Prepare for the souls you will be going to war over today. I want to hear about the seeds you plant and the victories you see. I also want to encourage you to journal during your time with God this morning and journal all the cool things God is speaking to you or using you to do today. You got this, soldier. Let's go, fight for some souls
- Captain Joshua.

Journal

Day 19

Get up, soldier. It is time to retreat from the enemy — day nineteen of our training and fighting. We cannot slow down now. Lives are at stake, marriages are at stake, souls are at stake, and if you don't get up and do something about it, who do you think will?

Today, we are focusing on the fact that our job is to team up with the Holy Spirit, and he leads us to go out into the harvest and bring in souls for the kingdom.

Read

Matthew 9:35-38

Listen

"Plead the Blood" by Cody Carnes.

Journal what the Lord speaks to you in your devotional time. Then, I want you to spend some time in prayer for the lost. Then do as this scripture says and pray to the Lord for more laborers to go out into the harvest and do the work. Today, your job is to be a harvester. I know it is hard, but it is your duty.

Share your story today of what God has done in your life with someone and how the Gospel of Jesus has impacted everything about your life. Then, ask them to join you for church on Sunday, and they can see what the Gospel of Jesus is all about. You got this, soldier. God is stretching you to make you more effective for his kingdom. Let's do this.

- Captain Joshua

Journal

Day 20

Get up, soldier. It's day 20, and it is time for your orders and training to start. This week's training has been about the importance of going after souls. People's souls are the most valuable thing we can spend our time, money, or energy on.

Read

Romans 3: 9-31

Listen

"Completely Abandoned" by Gateway Worship

Journal what you feel the Lord is sharing or challenging you with.

Now, I want you to abandon yourself and focus on what those scriptures are saying. Go out and do the work with God. I want you to invite three people or three families to join you for service this weekend. Use your training from this week and be led by the Holy Spirit.

Journal how the Lord uses you, who you invite, and what takes place. It is time for the church to be the laborers God has asked us to be. I can't wait to hear all about what God uses you to do. Also, do not forget we have pre-service prayer at 5 pm tonight and 9 am tomorrow. You need to be there if possible. It is a part of your training.

- Captain Joshua.

Journal

_____

_____

_____

_____

_____

_____

_____

_____

_____

_____

_____

_____

_____

_____

_____

_____

_____

_____

_____

_____

_____

_____

_____

Day 21

Wake up, soldier. I got great news for you. Today is day 21, which marks the halfway point for your basic training. Three weeks down, three weeks to go. You got this. Don't slow down; don't halfway do it. Let's let God stretch us and mature us. We are soldiers in the army of the Lord.

Listen

"So Will I" acoustic version by Tori Kelly (Best version ever)

Get your mind linked up with His. I want you to spend some time praying over people that you have been working on.

Open your journal and look at what God has been doing in you and speaking to you over the last three weeks. I would love for you to text me a testimony of what God is doing in you or what He has used you to do. Then I want you to get up and prepare for the 9 am prayer meeting if you come on Sundays. It is going to be a fantastic day

- Captain Joshua.

Journal

_____

_____

_____

_____

_____

_____

_____

_____

_____

_____

_____

_____

_____

_____

_____

_____

_____

_____

_____

_____

_____

_____

_____

Week 4

"Defending Against the Enemy"

Good day, Clawson family. For those of you who are just now joining us in this series, we are in the middle of one of the most incredible series of messages we have ever done here at Clawson. The title of the series is "The Battleship Church."

So far, The messages have been about recognizing the war around you and switching our mindsets from civilian to soldier, learning to get in shape, and using the weapons God has given you to use. This past week, Pastor Josh Rivera, a good friend, preached a message about the importance of the Gospel and the souls we are fighting for. How many of you were blessed by Pastor Josh Rivera last week? Amen.

Going back to the beginning of this series, a quote that shook me and started getting me ready to preach this series is, "The most valuable thing on this planet is a human soul, so much so that heaven and hell war over them daily. I felt like God said to me, "Josh, I need y'all to join that war."

Please check this out, all of you. How many of you guys in the room this morning have been drafted or enlisted into the Clawson boot camp that is going on right now? Right now, 256 people are going through boot camp. How many would say this boot camp is changing your life? Do you recognize the fight around you? Are you learning as you train to be more effective with your weapons? How many of you fought for some souls this week? AMEN, AMEN, AMEN, look at that. I believe God is raising an army here, and we are about to be more effective for the kingdom of God than we have ever been. Does anyone believe that?

Let me tell you something cool that I have never done before. My wife and I are taking all of the information from this series and putting it into a book. The chapters will be the messages being preached, then the six-week boot camp and all of the testimonies of what God is doing will be the book's last two chapters. If you have a remarkable testimony of what God has been doing in your life, I would love for you to send it to me via text so I can document it. So, hopefully, we can get that done pretty quickly, and you can take this home with you as a resource. I hope other churches and pastors will also get serious about building an army for Christ, and this book will be a resource to help them.

Alright, you all, it is time to dive into the content for today. As most of you probably know by now, our memory verse for this particular series is:

Matthew 28:19-20 New Living Translation

19 Therefore, go and make disciples of all the nations,[a] baptizing them in the name of the Father and the Son and the Holy Spirit. 20 Teach these new disciples to obey all the commands I have given you. And be sure of this: I am with you always, even to the end of the age."

You have two more weeks to recite that memory verse at the gift shop in the lobby, so make sure to get that done. Reciting your memory verses is a must if you are doing boot camp. Let's get them done, soldiers.

Again, we have talked about defining the war we are in, how to use our weapons, and the fight for souls. Today, if you are taking notes, the message's title is "Defending Against the Enemy."

You can turn to Ephesians 6 with me if you have your Bible. I am going to be reading a pretty large portion of scripture there. And then, we are going to dive into the message.

Ephesians 6:10-18 NLT

The Whole Armor of God

10. A final word: Be strong in the Lord and in his mighty power. 11 Put on all of God's armor so that you will be able to stand firm against all strategies of the devil. 12 For we[d] are not fighting against flesh-and-blood enemies, but against evil rulers and authorities of the unseen world, against mighty powers in this dark world, and against evil spirits in the heavenly places. (principalities, against powers, against the rulers of [b]the darkness of this age, against spiritual hosts)
13 Therefore, put on every piece of God's armor so you will be able to resist the enemy in the time of evil. Then, after the battle, you will still be standing firm. 14 Stand your ground, putting on the belt of truth and the body armor of God's righteousness. 15

For shoes, put on the peace that comes from the Good News so that you will be fully prepared.[e] 16 In addition to all of these, hold up the shield of faith to stop the fiery arrows of the devil.[f] 17 Put on salvation as your helmet, and take the sword of the Spirit, which is the word of God.

18 Pray in the Spirit at all times and on every occasion. Stay alert and be persistent in your prayers for all believers everywhere.[g]

If you are going to defend yourself, here are things that you need to keep in mind at all times:

The Enemy is Looking to Attack You at Your Weakest Moment, SO BE READY

That scripture told us to STAY ALERT. If you are not staying alert, you will not be able to defend yourself against the enemy because he isn't going to attack at your strongest. He isn't going to attack you when you are ready and looking out for the attack; he is going to attack at your weakest.

In the last couple of weeks, I have referenced the time Jesus was tempted in the wilderness by Satan, but today, I want to read you just a piece of that story. This is so important for you to understand.

Matthew 4:1-3 New Living Translation

4 Then Jesus was led by the Spirit into the wilderness to be tempted there by the devil. 2 For forty days and forty nights, he fasted and became very hungry.

3 During that time, the devil[a] came and said to him, "If you are the Son of God, tell these stones to become loaves of bread."

Everybody says during that time, during what time? Has anyone ever been there when Jesus was hungry and his physical body weak? When you are fasting, and you are just about to finish fast, and someone rolls into work with your favorite lunch, and not only that, but they brought you some during THAT time.

When Jesus was at his weakest physically and hungry, satan came to be his answer to his need.

Listen, Satan is sitting, he is watching, he is waiting.

1 Peter 5: 8

Stay alert! Watch out for your great enemy, the devil. He prowls around like a roaring lion, looking for someone to devour.

Has anyone ever watched how lions attack their prey? Here is what they do. They find a herd of something they want to eat for the day. They sit, wait, and watch, looking for the one that will be the easiest to catch. If there's a herd of wounded, smallest, or slowest, they'll go to watch and pick any one of them. Or, they will go after the ones that run off by themselves and do not stay under the protection of the herd. They aren't going after the ones that are all together, and they aren't going after the strongest. They go after the easiest one to pick off.

Listen to me; this is how satan is picking off Christian people left and right. He is stalking, watching, and looking for those who are not maturing in their faith. He is looking for people who are not very faithful, people who are isolated or not connected with the herd. You know what happens when a prey gets isolated; they get eaten. When he sees you at your weakest, he comes in to devour you, destroy your faith, tempt you to sin, and pull you away from those who are helping you be strong. You have to be ready to watch out for him to attack.

You must be closest to God in your weakest moments, rely on his strength, and stay with your herd. Your church family is the army God has placed around you.

Number 1: the enemy is looking to attack you at your weakest moment, so be ready.

Armor Up and Never Go Unprotected

Briefly, I want us to walk through the armor and what it looks like to armor up and be protected. So, the different armor pieces are the belt of truth, a breastplate of righteousness, shoes of peace, a helmet of salvation, a shield of faith, and a sword of the spirit.

So, let's walk through practically how I put on the armor of God and how I use it.

Belt of Truth

The way that you put on the belt of truth is to know the truth and to walk in truth. The only way to know the truth is to know the word of God. The Bible says that this is the truth. Listen to me, though. You can't just know it. You have to walk in it. James 1:26 tells us not just to be hearers of the word but doers of the word also. So, to wear my belt of truth, keep it on, and use it when deception comes my way, when lies come my way, when something that is a little twist of the truth comes my way, I cannot be deceived; I have to walk in the truth.

Hey, and can I be complex with you this morning? Anytime you willingly or accidentally lie and don't fix it right then, you remove your armor and open the door for the enemy. You are going unprotected when you lie. Telemarketer calls.

"Take off my belt." It's a little white lie that is not affecting anyone. "Take off my belt."

Listen, there is always a way out without a lie. The telemarketer calls, "Is Josh there?"

"He is unavailable."
"Is this Josh?"
"Yes, it is, and I am unavailable."
"Thank you, goodbye."

You don't have to lie. If you find yourself lying about stupid little things, know you are unprotected. Proverbs says there are six things God hates, seven that he detests, and second of the seventh is a liar. Keep your belt on. Know the truth and walk in truth.

Breastplate of Righteousness

In the armor of a Roman soldier, the breastplate served as protection for some of the most essential parts of the body. Underneath the breastplate is the heart, lungs, and other organs necessary for life. Therefore, if a soldier did not wear his breastplate, he was vulnerable to an attack that could result in instant death.

So, why does Paul call it the breastplate of righteousness? Suppose we do not protect ourselves with righteousness, our hearts with righteousness. In that case, we open ourselves up to attack from the enemy and can fall into sin that leads to death.

To be righteous means to obey God's commandments and live in a way that is honorable to Him. Psalm 106:3 says, "How blessed are those who keep justice, who practice righteousness at all times!"

Unfortunately, our sinful nature often gets in the way of living a righteous life. When we decide to live based on our own desires rather than God's, we are taking off Righteousness and making ourselves vulnerable to the enemy. Romans 8:6 says, "So letting your sinful nature control your mind leads to death. But letting the Spirit control your mind leads to life and peace."

So, the way to wear the breastplate of righteousness is to allow the righteousness of God to lead and guide your life and heart. If we take off God's righteousness and let Satan get to our hearts, we are in trouble in a way that will lead us to death.

Shoes of Peace

Used to, I would have told you that shoes were the least important part of an outfit, but boy, that has changed. Now I would say to most people they are the most important.

Think about what shoes do. They protect your feet, and they give us footing on insecure terrain. They help keep us steady when something unexpected hits us. Shoes ground us. Now, with the armor, they are called shoes of Peace.

Peace is freedom from disturbance or a state or period in which no war has ended. How can we have peace when there is a war going on? The only way is by understanding and knowing the gospel. The gospel of Jesus, learning the gospel of Jesus, and living by the gospel of Jesus are what give us footing in insecure terrain and keep us steady when something unexpected hits us. The gospel and our belief in the gospel are what ground us with peace, knowing that God has everything under control. You live in peace with the Gospel, and that keeps your shoes on for your armor.

Shield of Faith

We hold onto our faith like a shield. We have to choose faith in all circumstances deliberately. This means that when we encounter doubts or find a passage of Scripture that troubles us, we decide to hold on to faith.

So, how is faith like a shield?

A shield protects us from the arrows or blows from the enemy, a shield was also used to push back the enemy, and a shield was used when soldiers would get together to make a protective barrier.

Same thing in our faith. Our faith protects us when the enemy comes at us, and we choose faith over fear or deception. We are shielding ourselves from the enemy. Also, we use our faith to push back the enemy. Through faith, we cast out the enemy and trample on the enemy. And listen to me, you want real power when we join our faith together and build a protective wall against the enemy. We can do that with our faith. It is like a shield.

So, how do we take up the shield of faith? We pray that God will arm us with it in all circumstances, and we choose to take it up, even when the devil keeps firing arrows of doubt and deceit. And listen to me: when you have and see victories, focus on those victories, and your faith will have no choice but to grow.

Helmet of Salvation

It is pretty easy to know the importance of a helmet. It protects your head, mind, and brain. Where do you think your biggest battles happen? In your mind. So, how do I practically put on the Helmet of Salvation and keep it on? I have five things to do to protect your mind with the Helmet of Salvation.

Renew your mind in the word. Romans 12:1-2

Reject doubts that arise from circumstances.

Keep an eternal perspective - seek ye first the kingdom.

Capture your thoughts and stop evil thoughts from getting to your heart.

Remember that Victory is already accomplished.

Sword of the Spirit

The sword of the Spirit, God's word, is how you counterattack when attacked. We looked at this last week with Jesus and the Devil. When you know the word and satan comes at you, and you are protecting your heart and your mind. You have your feet ready with the Gospel and peace, and you can confidently take the word of God and slay the enemy with the truth. You can walk in the Authority of Christ, and you can win. Somebody shout amen.

The last thing I want to say about the Armor is this. I hear people say I wear my armor every morning when I wake up. I believe that is super cool and effective for the day, but when you say that, it sounds like you are not wearing your armor when you go to bed. And let me tell you something. Your mind and your heart need protection while you are sleeping. Which means you cannot afford ever to take your armor off. Once you put it on, you must wear it daily for the rest of your life. What you do is check it to make sure it is good. Is my helmet loose this morning? Are there areas the enemy could hit? Is my faith in a good place, my heart, my mind? Every morning, you secure and check it; every night, you do the same and use it all during the day. You need your armor on 24/7/365. If not, you will get hit and hurt.

Ok, so number 1 was that you need to understand that the enemy is looking to attack you at your weakest moments, so bet ready. Number 2 was to armor up and never go unprotected.

Surround Yourself with Allies Who Protect You

Probably another way to say this is to use your backup. The military has backup. Like Air support, you get yourself in a bind, pinned down, and if the enemy is on all sides, you can call in air support, give them the coordinates of the enemy, and watch them go kaboom. You got back up, and you got allies. The military has a thing no man left behind. I got your six soldiers and am here to fight with you and for you.

Countries have allies. America has lots of allies right now because of Israel's allies that are stopping other nations from wanting to join this war because if they attack Israel, their allies are going to join that war, too.

In the war you face, you have allies and backups you can call. So the question then becomes, who are your allies? Who do you call for backup and airstrikes in your time of spiritual warfare? You can't do it alone. You have God you can call on. You can ask for angels to come and aid you in war, but then you also have an army called the church of Jesus that is supposed to be there to be your backup.

Ecc 4:12 NLT

2 A person standing alone can be attacked and defeated, but two can stand back-to-back and conquer. Three are even better, for a triple-braided cord is not easily broken.

I brought someone up to push me to the ground. I did this with my eyes closed so I could not anticipate when or how hard the push would be

I need someone to come up here and help me. I want to show you something. I want you to understand the power of allies and backup.

Ok, yeah, that was painful. Look at me; this is what it looks like when you get hit with no backup. But Rylin and Kaynin came to help me. These are two of my sons, and they will provide some backup for me.

My sons got my back, so, hey, now, could you push me again? Have the boys catch me when I get hit this time. When someone has my back, I can get hit and not get hurt.

Now watch this. Boys, I need all of you to have my back still. You all got me. I trust you, ok. Watch this: satan's goal is to make you fall.

I brought my two sons up on stage. This time, when I was pushed, they could catch me when they did several trust falls throughout this segment

He wants you to fall back into sin. He wants you to fall into unbelief, and he wants to knock you down and make you fall where you cannot get back up. But that scripture said, "A person standing alone can be defeated." But what happens when we have backups? Here is what happens when Satan tries to make you fall. *(My sons continue to catch me. See images above)*

Boom! Listen, your backup catches you because they got your back. And it doesn't matter where you are going or what you are doing in life. If you got your backup around, you're going to be alright. Satan tries to make you fall for that woman, fall for pride and disbelief, fall into depression, or fall back into addiction. He tries every way to make you fall but listen to me when you have your backup, and they help catch you before you fall.

And listen to me, if you are going to pick a fight with Satan if you are going to be effective in the army of Christ, you need to know you are at war and you need your backup. You need some air support, and you need to holla at the prayer team. You need a shift in your mindset, and you need to holla at the worship team. You need some counseling and wise counsel. You need a mentor, and you need a miracle. Great, we have a team that believes and prayer for them, deliverance.

I will never understand why we have all these allies, and we could be winning the war for our minds and souls, and why so many Christians stay isolated and wind up falling. God put you in the army for you to have a backup, so use it.

Ok, so to protect yourself in this war, you need to understand that the enemy is looking to attack you at your weakest moments, so be ready. Number 2 was to armor up and never go unprotected. Every single day, check your armor and tighten your armor. And number 3, you surround yourself with allies who protect you.

You do those things, and you will learn to be super effective in the kingdom of God, and you will learn to be super effective in protecting those around you.

Response

Would you bow your heads and close your eyes? The practical way that I am going to ask you to respond to this message is by taking these pieces I gave you today and beginning to protect yourself, your marriage, your family, and your church.

But right now, what I am praying is that the Holy Spirit will do work in you right now. So, in just a moment, our worship team is going to lead us into a time of worship. If you are here and;

You are not following Christ; you have not joined his army, and today, you need to make things right with God.

If you are here, beaten down, tired, and worn out, you need strength and rest.

If you are here and you do not feel like you are being very effective in the army.

Would you step out and come if you need prayer for anything: healing, deliverance, peace, rest, or guidance?

If you would like to watch this message, please scan the QR Code below or visit Clawson.tv/battleship-church-four

DEFENDING AGAINST THE ENEMY

Results from the Message

The response to this message was mostly people wanting to come and get back up. People who have been doing boot camp are tired and worn out and want someone to provide backup to them in prayer.

I can tell that the enemy is striking our church family right now. In our Prayer meeting this morning and our service, the energy level was way lower than normal.

I believe the part of the prayer time this morning was a replenishment for those who are tired and weary and who need God to be their strength.

Day 22

Get up, soldier. There is a war around you, and it is time for you to get to training. Today is Day 22 of Boot Camp, and today, we will focus on Defending and Protecting ourselves with Truth.

Remember, the way to put on the Belt of Truth is to know the truth and to walk in it. So, let's take some time to get into our bibles this morning. Also, let's stop the practice of willingly lying about things that don't matter. Let's put our belts on and keep them on.

I want you to listen to "The Truth" by The Belonging Co. Read Philippians 4:4- 9 and 1 John 1:5- 10. Then, journal what you feel the Lord is sharing with you. I want you to be extra careful today. You are putting on your belt of truth, so satan will try to mess you up there. Be mindful of what you say, listen to, and trust. You got this, soldier. I got your back if you need me - Captain Joshua.

Journal

_____

_____

_____

_____

_____

_____

_____

_____

_____

_____

_____

_____

_____

_____

_____

_____

_____

_____

_____

_____

_____

_____

_____

_____

_____

_____

_____

_____

Day 23

    Ok, soldier, it is time to get up. I have let you sleep long enough. Day 23, and it is going to be a great day of training. Remember, this whole week, we are training on defending ourselves against the enemy. We are putting on the armor of God and checking it every morning and evening to ensure we are staying protected.

    The part of the armor that we will focus on today is the breastplate of righteousness. We cover our hearts and protect our hearts by living a righteous life. The life that God called us to live. When we live according to the flesh, and when we follow our earthly and sinful desires, then we are not wearing our breastplate and are not protected. Still, when we follow the leading of the Holy Spirit and the word of God and live righteously, we protect our hearts with the breastplate.

    Today, ensure your belt of truth is still fastened and walk in truth. And focus on righteousness today, living by the Word and the

Spirit. Put things not of God to death and live righteously in his eyes.

Read

Ephesians 6:10-20

Listen

"Cornerstone" by Bethel Music

Journal everything that God is speaking to you or challenging you with. You got this, soldier.

- Captain Joshua.

Journal

_____

_____

_____

_____

_____

_____

_____

_____

_____

_____

_____

_____

_____

_____

_____

_____

_____

_____

_____

_____

_____

_____

_____

Day 24

Good morning, soldier. Day 24 of Boot Camp, so get up and get ready for your training. Right now, check to ensure your belt of truth is fastened, and your breastplate of righteousness is tight and in place. You are walking in truth and walking in righteousness.

Today, we will focus on protecting our minds and putting on and keeping on the Helmet of Salvation. How do we protect our minds? It is by putting only good things into our minds. Romans 12 tells us to allow God to change the way we think. Here is the truth: our opinions, feelings, and what makes sense. It doesn't matter if it is not in line with God's mind and reality. So, today, we are focusing on shifting our minds to match God's word and not God's word to match our minds.

I want you to listen to Eden by Benjamin William Hastings and Read Romans 12:1-2, 2 Corinthians 10:3-5, and Philippians 4:8. Write in your journal what you feel God is sharing or challenging you with. Then today, I want you to protect your mind all day, Capture your thoughts, and think about the right things. Write a journal about your struggles, your thoughts, and the victories you are seeing. It is going to be a great day. Captain Joshua

Journal

_____

_____

_____

_____

_____

_____

_____

_____

_____

_____

_____

_____

_____

_____

_____

_____

_____

_____

_____

_____

_____

_____

_____

Day 25

Get up, soldier. It's day 25 of boot camp, and we have work to do. We don't have time to be sleeping. Before training today, you must check your mind and ensure it is protected with a helmet. Check your heart and make sure you are covered with the breastplate. Check and ensure you are studying truth, walking in truth, and knowing truth.

Now that you have that covered let's make sure we have peace on our feet from the Gospel. Sunday, I shared that when you understand the power of the Gospel and how it has impacted and transformed your life, you can have peace no matter the circumstances.

Read
Romans 10:9-13
Romans 1:16-17

Listen
"Peace" by Bethel Music and We the Kingdom

176

Journal what you feel the Lord is speaking to you. The goal is to put on your shoes by being confident in the Gospel you believe in. I got your back if you need anything or have any questions.

- Captain Joshua

Journal

Day 26

Good morning, soldier; here we go. It is
time to get up and ready for Day 26 of Boot
Camp. Do not get tempted to quit or stop; lives
are at stake. First, I want you to check the armor
you have on and ensure it is fastened the way it
needs to be. Ensure your mind and heart are
protected and walking in truth and peace.

Today, our focus is the Shield of Faith.
Faith is the substance of things hoped for, the
evidence of things not seen. You need to
understand all believers have been given a
measure of faith, and the goal is to grow in our
faith.

Read
Matthew 17:14-20
James 2:14-25
Hebrews 11

Listen
"Give Me Faith" by Elevation Worship

I want you to pray today that God will give you opportunities to grow your faith. Today, begin looking for those opportunities as He opens those doors. Make sure to journal what God is speaking to you in your devotional time. Journal the doors that open for your faith to be stretched. I would love to hear all about what He uses you to do. It is going to be a fantastic day, soldier

- Captain Joshua.

Journal

Day 27

Get up, soldier. It is time for a good spiritual workout. It is day 27 of your training, and I hope and pray that your spiritual health continues to grow and mature. Today, we are focusing on the last piece of the armor in Ephesians 6, and that is the Sword of the Spirit, the Word of God.

The word of God is the most valuable thing we have as believers besides the Holy Spirit. The Word keeps us in line with truth, and the Spirit empowers us to do the ministry. I know I always say this, but if you do not get into and dig into your word, you are fighting without a sword, without your most effective tool.

Read
Hebrews 4:12-13
2 Timothy 3:14-17
Psalms 119:105-112

Listen
"Word of God speak" by Big Daddy Weave

Today, I want you to practice attacking the enemy with the Word. If you don't have a scripture for the attack that is taking place, google one and strike back. Make sure to journal what God is speaking to you and what he uses you to do today. It is going to be a fabulous day.

Don't forget we have our pre-service prayer meetings tonight at 5 pm and tomorrow at 9 am. You need to be there if at all possible

- Captain Joshua.

Journal

Day 28

Get up, soldier. Now is not the time to get lazy! It is not the time to quit. You are ⅔ of the way through with your boot camp, and the goal is to finish strong and allow God to get you fully prepared for battle. Today is day 28. I want you to take some time this morning to reflect on this whole week.

We have spent the week putting on all six armor pieces and learning how to use them. Are you checking yourself in the morning to make sure you are ready for battle? Are you checking yourself to protect your heart and mind before sleeping?

Read
Ephesians 6

Listen
"Refiner" by Maverick City and Chandler Moore

After today, we will have a whole new training topic for next week, so make sure you are ready. If you have any testimonies or victories from this past week, I would love to hear and document them. Please send them to me. Don't forget we have a pre-service prayer at 9:00. I hope to see you then.

- Captain Joshua

Journal

Week 5

"Storm the gates of Hell"

What is up, Clawson Family? Is anybody ready to dig into the word of God? Ok, you all, well, it is about time to dive into what we are going to be looking at today. This series, to me, has just been pushing us forward and stretching us more every single week that we have gotten into it.

If you have not been here, I want to catch up with you quickly, and then I will dive into what we will discuss today. This is the fifth week we have discussed "The Battleship Church."

Week 1 was all about setting a foundation for the series in a message called "Defining the Fight." It was all about understanding the war that we are in—taking our mindset and moving from a civilian mindset to a soldier mindset. And to begin to have our spiritual eyes opened in our lives so we can see where the enemy is at work and where God is at work.

Week 2 was about "understanding your weapons" and using them. We reviewed the weapons of worship, prayer, and the word and discussed special operations training to get more extensive training in supernatural weapons.

Week 3 was all about the fact that the purpose of this war is the "souls" being fought for. We have a duty given to us by Jesus to share his life-changing Gospel with as many people as possible to restore people to God and see their souls get saved.

Week four of last week was about "Defending against the enemy." How do we defend ourselves, our families, our homes, and our church against the enemy? First, you must understand that the enemy will attack you at your weakest moment, so you must ensure you are ready. Secondly, you need to armor up and never go unprotected, and thirdly, you need to use your allies and call for backup.

Next week, we will close this series with a message called "Fight till the death." It will also be a celebration weekend; let me just say it will be a weekend you do not want to miss. Next week will also be the last day to say your memory verse for the month. Which is;

Matthew 28:19-20 New Living Translation

19 Therefore, go and make disciples of all the nations,[a] baptizing them in the name of the Father and the Son and the Holy Spirit. 20 Teach these new disciples to obey all the commands I have given you. And be sure of this: I am with you always, even to the end of the age."

You can recite that anytime at the Gift shop in the lobby. Now, it is time to dive into what we will be looking at today. If you are taking notes, the message's title is "Storm the Gates of Hell."

The purpose of this message is to help us understand that, as a church, it is not just our job to defend against enemy attacks. Still, God wants to use us to be offensive warriors and storm the gates of hell in warfare. Somebody shout amen. Now, how do we know that is a true statement? Because the word of God says;

Matthew 16:18 New King James Version

18 And I also say to you that you are Peter, and on this rock, I will build My church, and the gates of Hades shall not[a]prevail against it.

God's goal for the church is that the church becomes so powerful that we are pushing the powers of darkness back to hell and storming the gates. Just the thought of that gives me chills.

Listen to me: gates were what people put up to keep people out to protect their city. Gates are a defensive strategy. In the Bible, the City of David Jerusalem had an entire wall of defense around the city. It had these massive gates to keep the enemy out of the city and protect the people in the city. Babylon invaded that city, tearing down all the walls and burning the gates. The shame on God's people, because their gates of defense did not prevail was overwhelming.

Listen to me, I just picture in my mind the armies of Christ invading the defenses of Hell, tearing down the gates and shaming their defenses, and putting shame on the kingdom of darkness by the power of Christ and the kingdom of light, and that brings me so much joy.

So, is it possible for us to storm the gates of hell, and if so, how in the world do we accomplish that? If you are taking notes, number

1 in your notes is this. To storm the gates of hell, you have to understand.

You Can't Storm Anything Without Christ

Let me show you an example in scripture of someone trying to take on the enemy we are facing without Christ living in them and empowering them.

Acts 19:13-20 New Living Translation

13 A group of Jews was traveling from town to town, casting out evil spirits. They tried to use the name of the Lord Jesus in their incantation, saying, "I command you in the name of Jesus, whom Paul preaches, to come out!"14 Seven sons of Sceva, a leading priest, were doing this. 15 But one time when they tried it, the evil spirit replied, "I know Jesus, and I know Paul, but who are you?" 16 Then the man with the evil spirit leaped on them, overpowered them, and attacked them with such violence that they fled from the house, naked and battered.

I will never forget the most demonic encounter I ever got to experience here in the church at Clawson. I had someone call me and say to me, "Hey, pastor, my brother is full of demons, and I am bringing him to you to get them out." That type of thing happens, so I wasn't that alarmed. Usually, people exaggerate that type of thing quite a bit.

So they pulled up into the parking lot, and I walked outside and opened the door to the car. And he looks over at me, and he is growling, and there is what looks like blood coming from his mouth. Have you ever seen a dog with rabies? That is the best explanation, I think. I mean, he looked like a demon. So, I just very gently closed the door to the car, and I said nope. I'm not trying to do this by myself. So, what did I do? I called in some backup, as I talked about last week.

My mom and I, brother Finch, this guy's sister, and I think another person came to the church. We began to try to get this guy into a room at the church. Let me tell you something: it was like he had a supernatural strength. He threw me around the room, threw chairs across the room, and tried to bite us a couple of times. I mean, it was insane. I had never seen anything like this.

Luckily, I can say we did not end up like the sons of Sceva because we had the power of Christ inside of us, and after some crazy warfare, this guy got freedom, the demons got cast out, and he was back to normal. You could feel the shift in the room and in him when the demons left the room.

On another occasion, I heard a demon laugh at a team of prayer warriors praying over this lady to be free and tell them I have been in this family for 90 years. That family had continued to give this demon an open door in their family for decades. Why do I tell you this? For you to understand the enemy we are fighting is not a joke. If you go to take on that enemy without the power and authority of Christ, you just might end up Naked and battered.

We need to understand that satan has an army. We saw a list of that army last week.

Ephesians 6:12

12 For we do not wrestle against flesh and blood, but against principalities, against powers, against the rulers of [c]the darkness of this age, against spiritual hosts of wickedness in the heavenly places.

Remember I talked about the Army of God and how in the Army of God you have God who is commander and chief, then there are angels in the army of God, and there are different types of angels. There is the church, which holds God's power on earth. Officers in the church (Apostles, prophets, evangelists, pastors, and teachers) each have a specific job in equipping and training God's soldiers. Then there are soldiers, recruits, and boot campers. It is a huge army.

Listen, satan has an army, too. Some principalities are so powerful that their power and influence can extend over whole areas or even nations. Have you ever driven into a city and you could just feel the darkness? That is the power of a principality. Reynosa, Mexico, I feel that when I drive into that city. Then there are powers. If you go back to the Greek word here for powers, it is "exousia," which means "Delegated

Authority." A pretty high-ranking demonic spirit to whom satan has delegated authority to go and do his will against God. Then, the rulers of the darkness of the age would be like commanders. This one is over the army, this one is over the Air Force, this one is over the Marines, and so on. Lastly, there are spiritual hosts of wickedness in heavenly places. Lower-level evil spirits host wickedness in all forms, shapes, and sizes.

I hope you understand that satan hates you, and he hates God so much that he has structured and organized an army of Darkness to take you out, and you need to know. You don't have a chance and can't storm anything without Christ, which brings me to point number 2.

With Christ and His Authority, We Have the Power to Storm the Gates of Hell and Take on the Army of Darkness

In Matthew 28, Jesus commissions his troops and disciples and sends them out to do the work of the ministry, to take on the kingdom of Darkness. He wants them to understand the power and authority that has been given to him, which he, in turn, is giving to them.

197

Matthew 28:18-20 New Living Translation

18 Jesus came and told his disciples, "I have been given all authority in heaven and on earth. 19 Therefore, go and make disciples of all the nations,[a] baptizing them in the name of the Father and the Son and the Holy Spirit.20 Teach these new disciples to obey all the commands I have given you. And be sure of this: I am with you always, even to the end of the age."

He is telling them, "I am empowering you to take on the enemy." Let's look at Mark's version of this same event.

Mark 16:17-20 New Living Translation

17 These miraculous signs will accompany those who believe: They will cast out demons in my name, and they will speak in new languages.[a] 18 They will be able to handle snakes with safety, and if they drink anything poisonous, it won't hurt them. They will be able to place their hands on the sick, and they will be healed."

19 When the Lord Jesus had finished talking with them, he was taken up into heaven and sat down in the place of honor at God's right hand. 20 And the disciples went everywhere and preached, and the Lord worked through them, confirming what they said by many miraculous signs.

Listen, church fam, Romans 8 tells us that the same spirit that raised Christ from the dead is living in us.

As your captain, I need you to understand that you may be powerless against the enemy we are fighting without Christ, but when you give your life to Jesus Christ, when you become his disciple and walk in his authority, when you are filled with the Holy Spirit of God and the same spirit that raised Christ from the dead is living in you, all the demons, powers, rulers, principalities, evil spirit, the army of darkness doesn't stand a chance against the army of Christ.

Watch this: here is what can happen and what is beginning to happen in our pre-service prayer meetings before our services. We have learned to see the fight around us and how to spot the enemy and where he is working. We have now learned how to use our weapons and defend ourselves. So, what begins to happen is you get together with the army of Christ. You are in the battleship, and you are ready for war.

At this time, I jumped upon the battleship. Fired the cannons as I talked about firing on the enemy.

And in the spiritual realm, you can look and begin to see the enemy coming at the church, at your family, at your life. You have spotted him and see that he is coming to attack. Now, you get your weapons ready. Load the cannons, aim, lock on, and fire them when you see the next enemy coming. If we can sink that thing, snap aircraft carrier (principality). We are going to do some real damage. This time, load both cannons, aim, lock on, and fire. And together, we can take out the enemy with the power of Christ.

So, now, since you are a soldier who has been trained in warfare, your life is now about spotting the enemy, teaming up with the army of Christ, and using your weapons to take out the enemy, protect the army of Christ, and bring more souls into the Kingdom of God. This should be the work of the church in the world today. And this is the direction we are headed. Is anyone ready to storm the gates of hell? AMEN.

Ok, so number 1 was you can't storm anything without Christ, and number 2 was with Christ and his authority, we have the power to storm the gates of hell.

Storm the Gates in Prayer

Now, we have talked a lot about our different weapons. We have Worship, the word of God, prayer, and the gifts of the Holy Spirit. But I want to talk to you about strengthening your prayer life for a few minutes. There are tons of things that you can do to improve your prayer life. Just like you can learn to shoot a gun better and better, you can learn to be more strategic and effective in prayer.

Because of the training we have been doing, our prayer meetings before services have become much more strategic and powerful. People are learning to use discernment and their giftings. If you do not come to the prayer meetings and you are looking to grow and mature, you should. But here is what we have been doing there.

I got a whiteboard. And ask questions that I feel are led by the Holy Spirit for us to deal with.

Someone raise your hand and tell me an area in our church where you see God moving. OK, now, can someone tell me an area where you see the enemy moving in our church? According to scripture, someone else tells me what to pray and ask God for.

So, in this scenario, we have things that we need to celebrate and join with God in prayer over, we have areas that we need to fight against the enemy in the spiritual realm, and we have, according to the Bible, requests that we should make to God. This is simply using your discernment to work with God, work against the enemy, grab the bible, and pray in agreement with the word of God. This makes your prayers more powerful.

Three weeks ago, I felt God shared with me on Sunday that we needed to declare freedom over the spirit of offense. Then, in our prayer room, we really battled that spirit. Can I tell you what we have been doing spiritually is making a huge difference in our church? About 20-25 other pastors and I have joined together to begin to pray that the walls of division between churches and that religious spirit that is stopping the church from working together would be broken, and we are beginning to see that religious spirit released from this area. There is power in your prayers when you decide to listen to the Holy

Spirit, join the army of Christ, and storm the gates of hell in prayer. There are some other things that I think are so important for you to put into practice if you are going to be the most effective in your prayers.

Fasting

What is fasting? Fasting is giving up something physically to gain momentum in the spiritual. Most people say if you're not fasting food, then you're not fasting, but according to 1 Corinthians 7:5, you can also fast sex, and there are even different types of food fasts.

Why would you fast? To give up something physical that you love to grow with God and grow your spiritual muscles.

According to scripture, your prayers are more powerful when you are fasting to the lord. In Matthew 17, they tried to cast a demon out of a boy but were unsuccessful. Jesus tells them it was because of their faith that they were unsuccessful. Then, in verse 21, he says, "However, this kind does not go out except by prayer and fasting."

For those of you in boot camp or those who are looking to grow spiritually, I am asking our church family to join in for a corporate fast starting tonight at 6 pm and going until next Sunday at 6 pm. I am asking you to choose from 4 different kinds of fast food.

Complete fast - just water or liquids.

Daniel fast - fruits, veggies, and nuts.

Intermediate fast - eat one time a day and fast the other two meals

Complete secular fast - where you are not putting any secular news, shows, music, or anything else into your mind.

B. Declaring in Prayer

I think it is essential for you to understand that as a child of God, you do not have to beg God, like a little child begging their parents for something. Lord, please do this thing for me. Not that you shouldn't ask God for things. You should ask God for things; there is power in your asking God for things. Hezekiah was supposed to die, and he asked God not to allow him to die yet, and God gave him 15 more years to live. But I think we should also understand the power of declaring things in the name of Jesus.

Listen to me - you live a life in obedience to Him, you listen to the spirit of God and what He is leading you to do, and then you can declare for things to be done in the name of Jesus.

Mark 11:22-23 New Living Translation

22 Then Jesus said to the disciples, "Have faith in God. 23 I tell you the truth, you can say to this mountain, 'May you be lifted up and thrown into the sea,' and it will happen. But you must really believe it will happen and have no doubt in your heart.

You need to understand that if you declare something or even ask for something and are not living in obedience, your disobedience is causing curses and taking power from your prayers. Also, saying something that the Holy Spirit did not lead you to do doesn't mean you will receive it. The Bible is not a name. It claims its Gospel. I can't name, claim, or declare a 2023 Corvette and expect God will give it to me. In John 5, Jesus said.

John 5:19 New Living Translation

19 So Jesus explained, "I tell you the truth, the Son can do nothing by himself. He does only what he sees the Father doing. Whatever the Father does, the Son also does.

So, when we declare what the Father wants us to say and what he is doing in Jesus's name, there is power in our declarations. We have been declaring things against the enemy and seeing them come to pass because the spirit of God is leading us to declare them. So, align yourself with God and what he is doing, and allow him to use you to assert his power. That is what Jesus did.

Then, the last thing I wanted to share to strengthen your prayer life was.

C. Intercession

A few weeks back, I gave our prayer team a word that God was raising intercessors in our team and that God would begin to wake them up in the wee hours of the morning for them to go to war in prayer.

The next week, I asked how many of them had been waking up in the middle of the night and praying, and 17 of them raised their hands. I believe in our church; God is raising up intercessors.

To intercede means to intervene on behalf of another. So, intersession is going to God on behalf of another person, a group, or a church. So, when God wakes them up in the middle of the night, I am asking them to intercede on behalf of the Church family.

Have you ever felt the need inside you or were burdened to pray to God for someone? That is intercession.

So, I am asking you guys to join me in fasting, to begin to practice declaring the word and what the spirit gives to you, and to begin interceding on behalf of the church.

Suppose we do those things together in unity as a church family. In that case, you have no idea what we are about to do in the spiritual realm as we are pushing back the darkness and storming the gates of Hell in the name of Jesus.

Response:

Worship Team, would you come, and the Altar team, while they are getting ready, would you guys come and begin to pray?

In just a second, our worship team will lead us in worship as they do if you need prayer.

Maybe you are here and need to get things right with God.

Maybe you are here and need to be filled with the Holy Spirit.

You are here, and your spirit is down. You are tired and weary.

You are here and need something supernatural from God: healing, deliverance, guidance, and peace.

Or if you just want to come and pray or worship the lord, would you come?

If you would like to watch this message, please scan the QR Code below or visit Clawson.tv/battleship-church-five

Results from the Message

Very cool results from this message. We had about 50% of the church commit to fasting the next seven days for the boot campers, for the lost, for our upcoming celebration service, and for our miracle night that is taking place next Sunday night.

I also want to say that we have a pre-service prayer meeting on Saturdays at 5 pm and Sundays at 9 am. It is about a 50-minute, very strategic prayer meeting. Part of the results of this boot camp has been from averaging about 25 people in our prayer meetings to over 60 people who are now showing up and going to war in prayer.

Day 29

Get up, soldier. It is time for Day 29 of Boot Camp. This week is all about storming the gates of hell in prayer and being more effective in your prayer life.

Don't forget, we have started a seven-day fast. Fasting is giving up something physically to gain momentum in the spiritual. This fast is a part of your boot camp, so skipping it is not an option.

Read
Philippians 4:4-9
Mark 11:22-26

Listen
"More than Able" by Elevation Worship

I want you to grab your journal and write down where you see God working in your life or your family, and then I want you to write down where you see the enemy's attack. I want you to spend some time today aligning yourself with God, thanking him for what he is doing, and then attacking the enemy in prayer where you see him working. You got this, soldier. Storm the gates of hell

- Captain Joshua.

Journal

Day 30

Good morning, soldier. It is time to get up and start doing your training for Boot Camp day 30. As of today, you have made it through a month of boot camp. This means if you have been doing this right, your life and mind should be totally different from 30 Days ago.

Don't forget to fast, pray, and give up things in the physical to gain momentum in the spiritual. Today, I want us to train on intercession. Interceding for someone means intervening on behalf of another or standing in the gap for them.

Listen
"More like Jesus" by One Voice Worship.

I want you to take out your journal, and as the Holy Spirit gives you people or groups of people to intercede for and pray over, I want you to write that in your journal. I want you to spend your day today listening for the Holy Spirit to direct you to people to pray for. You write them down and intercede for them. It is going to be an awesome day. Don't quit; we have less than two weeks left. Let's finish strong

- Captain Joshua.

Journal

_____

_____

_____

_____

_____

_____

_____

_____

_____

_____

_____

_____

_____

_____

_____

_____

_____

_____

_____

_____

_____

_____

_____

_____

_____

Day 31

Get up, soldier. It is time to align ourselves with God, defend ourselves, our families, and our church against the enemy, and storm the gates of Hell. It is day 31 of Boot Camp training. Today, I want you to train in praying to the lord by asking and declaring.

In the scriptures, we pray to God because he tells us to ask, and you shall receive, seek, and you shall find knock, and the door will be opened. He also tells us that he has given us the authority to cast out demons and tramp on the enemy.

Read
Matthew 7:7-12
Matthew 28:16-28
Mark 16:15-20

Listen
"He is in the Room" by Tasha Cobbs or David Jennings.

I want you to spend some time in the Word and listen to the Holy Spirit. Begin to declare things over yourself, your family, and your church. Write down the things that you are declaring in your journal. Write down what the Lord is speaking to you. What he leads you to speak and declare all day today. Going to be a great day. You got this, soldier.

- Captain Joshua

Journal

Day 32

Get up, soldier. It is time for Day 32 of Boot Camp. You have made it halfway through the fast. Please be in prayer for celebration weekend and Miracle Night this weekend. I believe the words the Lord gave me for Miracle Night are "Signs and Wonders." Would you be praying with me about that?

This week is all about storming the gates of hell in prayer, strengthening your prayer life, and attacking the enemy in prayer.

Read
 Matthew 6:5-18
 2 Chronicles 7:14-15

Listen
"Promises" by Maverick City

Today, I want you to intercede on behalf of our nation. Pray that we would turn back to God and He would heal our land. Then pray and negotiate for the weekend services this week. Lastly, if you have a Facebook, I want you to share the Clawson Facebook post about this week's gun giveaway. Let's see if we can get some new faces in the church to hear the word. Journal everything that God is doing and sharing with you. I got your six, soldier. It is going to be a great day

- Captain Joshua.

Journal

_____

_____

_____

_____

_____

_____

_____

_____

_____

_____

_____

_____

_____

_____

_____

_____

_____

_____

_____

_____

_____

_____

_____

_____

_____

_____

_____

Day 33

Get up, soldier. It is time for day 33 of Boot Camp. It is time to storm the gates of hell, to take on the enemy, and to defend our families and church.

Read
Mark 2:1-12
Luke 8:40-56

Listen
"Tear off the roof" by Brandon Lake

During your time reading, I want you to journal what the Lord is revealing or speaking to you.

Now I want to ask you the question: how desperate are you for a move of God in your life? How desperate are you to see God do something supernatural in your life or a person you know? Miracle night this Sunday Night. The theme is Signs and Wonders, and I want to encourage you to come and receive from God. I want you to stretch your faith and bring someone you know needs to receive from God. It is time for us to get to work, soldier. I got your back. Let's go

- Captain Joshua.

Journal

Day 34

Get up, soldier. It is Day 34 of Boot Camp, and I could not be more excited about your training today and the services for this weekend. We have Celebration services on Saturday at 6 pm and Sunday at 10:30 pm. We will celebrate the boot campers, so you don't want to miss it.

Today, for your training, I want you to put together all this week's training and put it all into action. I want you to intercede as God leads you for different people and groups. I want you to declare what God is leading you to or what you find in the Word. I want you to enhance your prayers by fasting, aligning yourself with God, and attacking the enemy.

Read
  Colossians 3:1-17

Listen
  "If I Could Have Anything" by House Fires.

Journal what God is speaking to you. I want you to storm the gates of Hell in prayer today. Spend some extra time in prayer. Pray for our services this weekend, and pray for Miracle Night. We have prayer today at 5 pm or tomorrow at 9 am. You need to try to be at one of those if possible. You got this, soldier. Don't let up; let's push back the enemy's forces.

- Captain Joshua

Journal

Day 35

LET'S GO, BOOT CAMPERS: Day 35 of boot camp—your last day of training before our six days of reflection and putting this whole training to work. Next week will be the last week of training from me, but it will be all about putting all of your training into action. We will focus on it all.

Today, I want you to storm the gate, which is hell for our services. Today is the last day to fast, and I want you to focus on interceding for the lost people coming to services today, the sick and broken that are coming to Miracle Night tonight. I believe in miracles.

Read
Romans 14

Listen
"Revival's in the Air" by Bethel Music.
"House of Miracles" by Brandon Lake.

Journal what you feel God is speaking to your spirit. Then I hope to see you at prayer at 9:00 am. You guys are killing it

- Captain Joshua.

Journal

_____

_____

_____

_____

_____

_____

_____

_____

_____

_____

_____

_____

_____

_____

_____

_____

_____

_____

_____

_____

_____

_____

_____

_____

Week 6

"Fight Till Death"

What is up, Clawson Family? I do not have much time today, but I would like to share what is on my heart for just a few minutes. Today, we are closing out the series of messages that we have been in for what seems like forever. Y'all help me out; what is the name of the series? "The Battleship Church". We have a saying here at Clawson, "This church is a battleship, not a cruise ship," this series has really been about what it looks like to join the army of Christ and be a battleship church.

Week 1, we defined the war and fight going on and began to recognize the work of the enemy and the work of God around us. In week 2, we learned how to use the weapons God gave us to fight the enemy. Week 3, we talked about the whole reason we do what we do is for souls, to see more souls in Heaven and fewer souls in hell. Week 4 was all about defending against the enemy. Last week was probably my favorite of all of the messages, "Storm the Gates of Hell," today, I will close this thing out with a message titled "Fight till Death."

This is just a reminder that today is the last day you can say your memory verse at the Gift shop, so make sure to get that done.

Matthew 28:19-20 New Living Translation.

Would you stand with me as we get ready to dive into this last message, and can we pray together that God would give us exactly what we need to hear from him today?

Prayer

I have been praying. God, what do you want me to cover in this last message? And I felt like God gave me three things. Maybe for some of you, these will be reminders, but three things are essential for us to understand as we battle in the army of Christ. And this first one I have just felt all week in my spirit. I have probably mentioned it at some point in the series, but this week, this has been all over me.

I Fight Demons, Not People

I love our new shirts; I fight demons.

Ephesians 6:12 New Living Translation

12 For we[a] are not fighting against flesh-and-blood enemies, but against evil rulers and authorities of the unseen world, against mighty powers in this dark world, and against evil spirits in the heavenly places.

I need you to hear me, Church family. If you will be effective in this war, you must be fighting the right thing. If you fight the demons, spirits, evil forces, and armies of darkness, you will be very effective for Jesus. And draw people back to God. But hear me out, and this has been in my spirit this week, "If you fight people, you are going to not only be ineffective for Christ, but you will push people away from Christ." You will do the opposite of what your heavenly father desires. The Bible says, "He is trying to draw all men to him, so we need to make sure that we are aligning ourselves with what god is doing and are not pushing any men away from Him." No matter how evil or wrong those men or women are.

I believe that you can have the right heart, the right desire to stand for your God, and the right intentions. And without realizing it, you can work against God by standing against people and making their hearts even harder towards the Gospel. I don't want you to misunderstand what I am saying. We should always stand against sin, all Sin, and we should always stand on the truth. And sometimes, when you stand against sin and for truth, people think you are standing against them, but you are standing against the influence the enemy has on them.

But every person has a soul, and my goal should always be, no matter the person, to attack the enemy's influence on this person and influence them to receive Jesus and see the truth.

Listen to me; witches are not my enemy. They are people with souls, and I have seen Witches get saved and become very effective for the Kingdom of God. Satanists are not my enemy. It seems like they are, but they are not; they have souls, and just like satan's goal is their soul, God's goal is their soul. God does not want them to go to hell, and we should not either. Satanists have come to know the truth and have been able to help the army of God come against the army of satan. People who decide to let their kids dress up for Halloween or, God forbid, take their kids trick or treating are not the enemy. In the last few weeks, I have seen all the posts about celebrating Halloween and allowing your kids to dress up or not. All the bickering and arguing with people on Facebook is not doing you any good. So, how do I decide what I am or what I am not going to do?

Colossians 3:23-24 New King James Version

23 And whatever you do, do it heartily, as to the Lord and not to men, 24 knowing that from the Lord you will receive the reward of the inheritance; for[a] you serve the Lord Christ.

You can judge me if you want to. I don't care. I don't celebrate Halloween. I'm not too fond of it, but I take my daughter downtown most years and allow her to go to the businesses to get candy and dress up. You know what I am doing while she is doing that: being a light in the darkness. Doing it as unto the Lord, share the love of Christ, and if you don't like that. It's ok. But we don't have to argue about it. You do whatever you do unto the lord, and I will do the same—using where I am as a mission field.

If we spent half as much energy loving and reaching people as we do arguing about stuff online, we would probably attract many more people to Jesus just by being Jesus and following his example.

Don't make the mistake of pushing people into your enemy. It is the Demonic influence over their life that we fight, but the people, through the presence of God and the love of Christ, are called to reach. So, number 1 was I fight demons, not people.

Take Back What the Enemy Stole from You

When I say that, it makes me think of that old song. I went to the enemy's camp and returned what he stole from me. Do any of you remember that song?

Truth is we see it all in scripture that we serve a restoring God. Job had everything taken from him, and God restored it and gave him double. Israel, multiple times when they turned away from God, had everything taken from them, even themselves put into slavery, and God restored that nation time and time again. Abraham had a lot restored. David defeated the Amalekites and took back everything that they had stolen. I want to read you a verse from this story cause I think it is so cool.

1 Samuel 30:18-19 New King James Version

18 So David recovered all that the Amalekites had carried away, and David rescued his two wives. 19 And nothing of theirs was lacking, either small or great, sons or daughters, spoil or anything which they had taken from them; David recovered all.

Can I give you an encouraging word this morning? God can restore and recover even the things you have thought impossible for him.

"Pastor, my marriage is over. It is unrestorable."

That is if you do not allow God to restore it. Otherwise, it can be restored — my child, parents, finances, health, mind. I want you to hear me.

Satan is the one who convinces us that these things cannot be restored because if we lose hope and don't have faith, they may never be restored. But everyone says that if you put your hope and faith in God and walk out his will for your life, you can take back the things the enemy stole, and God can restore and recover it all.

So, what in your life right now do you need to take back from the enemy? Your marriage, relationship, sobriety, mind, finances, or health? Where do you need to see God move in a supernatural way to restore what Satan has taken in your life?

My biggest restoration story is my life restored to God. But a close second was my marriage when I got saved. Yall, I was stupid before I came to Jesus or anyone else, and I never thought my wife would trust me again. And I want you to hear me. It took months after I gave my life to Jesus for God to restore our marriage. She didn't speak to me for months; for four months, I lived in a different part of the house than her. BUT GOD, everybody says, 'But God,' he restored our marriage, and we will celebrate 20 years of marriage next year.

Don't you tell me he can't do it because I know he can. I will say this, and then I am going to move on. It is a lot of work if you are unwilling to work and fight and are unwilling to do your part. God may not do his part. So don't quit. Keep up the fight, and take back what the enemy has stolen. Ok, now to number 3.

Finish the Race Strong

Fight till Death

2 Timothy 4:6-8 NLT Paul tells Timothy...

6 As for me, my life has already been poured out as an offering to God. The time of my death is near. 7 I have fought the good fight, I have finished the race, and I have remained faithful. 8 And now the prize awaits me – the crown of righteousness, which the Lord, the righteous Judge, will give me on the day of his return. And the prize is not just for me but for all who eagerly look forward to his appearance.

The prize is for those who don't give up, those who finish the race, and those who keep fighting the fight until they go to be with Jesus.

According to Revelation 12:10, satan is going to fight for your soul until your last breath. It says, "The accuser is not stopping and never going to stop accusing us." No peace treaty is ever going to be signed. "Day and night he accuses us," the Bible says. Day and night, he is trying to take us out. So, even when it gets tiring, even when we are worn out, even when we are getting older, even when we feel like we have nothing left, we have to continue to stand, continue to armor up, continue training the generations coming up underneath us, continue to fight, and God will give us the strength to do it.

I thought of all kinds of biblical examples to use for fighting till death, but briefly, I want us to look at two examples in the Bible and how differently they were fighting, but they both fought till they died.

Stephen, in the book of Acts, was one of them. Stephen was stoned for preaching the word of God. Maybe he should have been less offensive with his words, But I think Stephen was more concerned about giving them the truth than he was being offensive. So, they drugged him outside the city and began to stone him.

Acts 7:59-60 New Living Translation

59 As they stoned him, Stephen prayed, "Lord Jesus, receive my spirit." 60 He fell to his knees, shouting, "Lord, don't charge them with this sin!" And with that, he died.

Tell me he was not focused on souls until the end, Lord. Don't charge them with this sin. He fought for souls literally until his last breath.

Another example that may hit more home since most of us will probably not get stoned for preaching the truth is David. In 1 Kings Chapter 2, as David is on his deathbed, he brings Solomon, his son, in to ensure he finishes his race, and he tells Solomon. Remember, the most important thing you can do is follow the commands of the Lord and learn to know God intimately. Then he gives him a list of all of the things Solomon needs to know so that everything David worked his life on would get done, and then he dies. But he was focused on the work of the Lord until he gave his last breath. He ensured he finished his race, and his son would take the baton and keep going.

When William B Travis was fighting in the Alamo and was about to be overthrown by Santa Anna, He wrote a letter to the people of Texas and all Americans. He knew without help, he and his men were about to lose this battle. But in this letter, he writes.

"The enemy has demanded a surrender at discretion. Otherwise, the garrison will be put to the sword if the fort is taken. I have answered the demand with a cannon shot, and our flag still waves proudly from the walls. I shall never surrender or retreat."

Church family, in the spiritual, this has got to be our answer to the enemy. To answer him with shots fired, and our Banner raised high, that we will never surrender or retreat. We will fight to the death and finish the race the Lord has laid before us.

Response:

Would you stand with me today? Worship team, would you get ready to lead us in worship? Altar team, would you come and begin to pray?

Church family, would you bow your heads and close your eyes? The message this morning is to fight to the death. I fight demons, not people. Remove what the enemy has stolen and finish the race. I believe with all my heart that God wants to work in you this morning if you allow him to.

As I was getting ready to preach this message this morning, I just felt like the response to the message was for us to make a fresh commitment to God.

Maybe that is a fresh commitment to follow him and make things right with God today.

Maybe that is a commitment that you will not fight people, but you will align yourself with God and fight demons to win people.

Maybe for you, today is committing to start to take back what the enemy has stolen.

Or to commit to God to fight to death and finish the race he has laid before you.

With every head bowed and every eye closed, would you raise your hand if you feel like God is challenging you and encouraging you to make a fresh commitment to him in one or more of these areas? And I would like to pray for you.

Thank you for raising your hands; here is what I want to ask as I prepare to pray and our team gets ready to lead us. I would love for us as a church family to come down to the altar, find a place to commit those things to God, allow him to do new work in us, and speak to us today. So right now, as I pray, if you are making a new commitment to God, would you step out and come and find a place to do that and give him some time to speak to you and minister to you?

If you would like to watch this message, please scan the QR Code below or visit Clawson.tv/battleship-church-six

FIGHT TILL DEATH

Results from the Message

The church did become a house of prayer at the end of this message. Lots and lots of people came to the altars, made seats out of their altars, and made new, fresh commitments to God.

What is crazy is that right now, part of the results of this series is that everyone is wondering what is next. We are done with boot camp, so what is next? So, at the moment, I am writing a special ops training for the boot campers. Until then, I will continue to provide daily training for them.

Day 36

Alright, soldiers, it is Day 36 of boot camp. This last week will be about putting together all the training we have been doing.

Today, I want you to focus your heart and mind on the war we are fighting. I want you to see where God is working and align yourself with him. Either to pray for someone or to witness to them. I want you to see where the enemy is working, to be in the spiritual attack, and to pray against the enemy's influence in their lives. But in the physical, it is to love them and show them kindness to draw them to Christ.

Read
Ephesians 3:14-21

Listen
"Adoption" by Brandon Lake.

Then, journal what the Lord is giving you this morning. It is going to be an amazing day. You got this, soldier

- Captain Joshua.

Journal

Day 37

Get up, soldier. I don't know what you are doing sleeping. A war is happening around you, and it is time for you to get involved. This is Day 37 of training. You have five days left, and it is up to you to finish Strong.

As you get up today, I first want you to check your armor. How are you doing in your mind? How is your heart? Are you ready with the Gospel of Peace? ARE YOU WEARING YOUR BELT OF TRUTH? Get your armor in place and fastened. Today is going to be a day of mediation.

To intercede for someone, you need to be in the right place mentally and spiritually, which is why the armor is necessary. I was hoping you could listen to the Holy Spirit as he is directing you. I want you to combat the forces of Darkness by aligning yourself with God and attacking the enemy's influence as God directs you.

Read
Matthew Chapter 5

Listen

"Count EM" by Brandon Lake

"Spirit Lead Me" by Influence Music and Michael Ketterer

Write in your journal what the Lord is speaking to you. Spend your day today listening to the Holy Spirit and interceding on behalf of people. It's going to be a great day. YOU GOT THIS SOLDIER

- Captain Joshua.

Journal

_____

_____

_____

_____

_____

_____

_____

_____

_____

_____

_____

_____

_____

_____

_____

_____

_____

_____

_____

_____

_____

_____

Day 38

It is day 38 of BOOT CAMP. Get up and get ready for training. We don't have time for you to sleep. Today will be a day where we focus all our attention on the Souls around us. Remember, we fight demons, not people, and we save people from hell.

Read
Matthew Chapter 6

Listen
"Rooftops" by Jesus Culture ft. Kim Walker.

Journal what God is speaking to you. Today is going to be a day proclaiming that we are His. Claiming with our lives that we are Jesus's people.

I want you to spend your day today looking for people you can influence as Jesus did. Pray for people, cast out demons, heal the sick, and show his love. Come pray against the enemy and help God draw souls to himself. It is going to be an amazing day for the Kingdom of Jesus. I would love to hear all about what God uses you to do.

- Captain Joshua

Journal

Day 39

ONLY 3 DAYS LEFT. Get up. It is time to get busy. Day 39 of BOOT CAMP is time to partner with God's people coming against the enemy. Let's bring down heaven and storm the gates of hell.

Read
Matthew chapter 7

Listen
"What your mercy did for me" by Indiana Bible College.

Journal the things that God is speaking to you and revealing to you. Over the last three days, you have read over the most famous sermon of all time, the Sermon on the Mount.

In this sermon, Jesus shifted our mindset from having our minds on the physical to having our minds on the spiritual. This series has been about God opening our eyes to the Spiritual around us.

Today, I want you to focus on having an eternal mindset in what you do. Look for the work of the enemy and come against him. Look for the work of God and align with him. Keep your armor on, and focus on reaching and loving people in your everyday life. That is God's will for us. Let's do this, soldier. You got it

- Captain Joshua.

Journal

Day 40

Day 40 of Boot Camp: Get dressed, get your phone, bible, and journal, and it is time for training. Today, I want you to focus on my first point from this past week's message. I fight demons, not people.

I think this is an enormous challenge for us. We desire to stand up for God; sometimes, in doing so, we stand against people instead of demons and push people away from God.

Read
Matthew chapter 18

Listen
"Reckless Love" by Bethel Music

As you read and God speaks to you through the Word, I encourage you to journal what he says. Today, I want you to focus on God's lost sheep. Let's have the same reckless love for them that God has for us.

I believe God will open doors for you today to share his reckless love and be the hands and feet of Jesus. Make sure you open your spiritual eyes to see and hear Him whenever He directs you. Now get to work, Soldier.

- Captain Joshua

Journal

Day 41

Get up, soldier. It is time for training: BOOT CAMP day 41. Today, I want your focus entirely on taking back what the enemy has stolen from you.

First of all, I want you to sit and reflect on things that the enemy has stolen from your life, and in your journal, I want you to write those things down. As time passes, I want you to be able to go back to this list and watch as God restores stuff in your life.

Read
Joel 2:25-26
1 Peter 5:10

Listen
Enemies Camp by Lindell Cooley
"Can you believe what the Lord has done in me" by Lindell Cooley

Today, I want you to begin to pray and believe in restoration. Journal what you feel God is giving you to pray. Get ready, and we have our last day tomorrow

- Captain Joshua.

Journal

Day 42

Today is the last day of BOOT CAMP! You have stayed with me for 42 days now. Six weeks. First of all, I want to thank you for being serious about God's Kingdom and joining the army of Christ.

Listen
"Crowns Down" by Gateway Worship.

Now, I want you to sit and read over the journal you have been writing in. Reflect for a few minutes on what God has done in your life over the last six weeks.

Then, if you are open to it, I would love for you to text me testimonies of what this boot camp has done in your life over the last six weeks. I will share some of these in the book I am writing, so please let me know if you do not want me to share. Thank you so much for graduating from Boot Camp. Keep up the good work, soldier

- Captain Joshua.

Journal

TESTIMONY TIME

Testimonies From Bootcamp

Testimonies

"Good morning, Captain. I'm extremely excited about this being drafted. I always knew there was a spiritual warfare, but I didn't know how to recognize that's what it was, or maybe I was just flat out seeing things in the flash and reacting to that. In the last few days, I recognized a lot, and I try hard not to react to it but pray about it. Thank you for doing this and teaching us more about the Bible, more about ourselves, and more about spiritual warfare. You rock, Josh, so keep doing what you're doing," said Chasity Bailey.

"Last night, as I was praying, I was baptized with the holy spirit for the first time, and it was such an amazing blessing to me," said Cody O'quinn.

"I am so grateful for this teaching/training. This week, I've fallen deeper in love with the Almighty and have greater gratitude for what He's done for me, in me, and through me. I'm gaining increased confidence and authority in who I am and what I carry because of Him. Unexpected blessings. But also insight into the spiritual realm of warfare. No small thing. Thank you for leading us well. You are appreciated," said Becky Wells.

"Last week, satan attacked my mind big time. I couldn't concentrate on reading the Bible or worshipping. Just thoughts of things to do, etc., would not stop. The only thing I knew to do was to tell Satan to get behind me in the name of Jesus. It is so new to me because I'm not naturally a fighter. I've hit someone once in my life, and that was my cousin. I'm going to use the weapons you preached about, though. It's really about figuring out how to get to the place to allow God to fight, right?" said Sheila Whitaker.

"For the first time in forever, I recognized a temptation and stopped myself before I fell for it! Maybe too much information, but I have struggled with bad anxiety my whole life, and today, I was able to catch myself before I fell for the temptation to try and do it all on my own this morning," said Amanda Holster.

"Hey friend, I woke up this morning literally two minutes before my 4 AM alarm, which is completely unheard of. I'm usually sleeping until 6 AM on a good day, lol. The Lord said, "Stay up and go to war for your family." Anyway, I decided to catch up on all the boot camp prompts!!! Honestly, I haven't been staying on top of it, and I had no intentions of starting, but holy heck, I'm so glad that I did. These past few weeks have honestly just been hell for me spiritually. I feel like I'm being attacked from every angle possible. This boot camp was what I needed and has brought me so much peace. I also just wanted to say thank you. I am truly just so blessed to get to call you my pastor. Thank you for letting the Holy Spirit guide you. Thank you for meeting people where they are right in the middle of their mess. Nothing scares you; you live boldly and are what this Kingdom needs. You are, without a doubt, right where you need to be. Love you, dude!"

- A.S.

"I have a praise report! God is so good! Stacy and I prayed very specifically yesterday about something, and God was fixing it as we were praying about it! Then, he showed it to me and said, you know I have this handled. Satan loves to stir up my anxiety!! God said, take a deep breath. Thank you for allowing God to work in you!!! There is something extraordinary going on in the church! It has really been a breakthrough for Stacy and me," said Cindy Davenport.

"Good morning, Pastor! I just wanted to thank you for being the real deal. This boot camp has woken me up in places I didn't realize I had been asleep. I homeschool my kids, and the first thing they do is get in the word and journal about what God has shown them or tell me if they can't write yet. Lol, anyhow, I felt I needed to enroll my 17-year-old in boot camp. So she's on day three and LOVES IT!! Also, yesterday, I went to Home Depot to get more hardware cloth for the chicken coop I'm building. I don't know much at all about tools. So I needed help finding the right staples, and there was a man who came to help. I felt sorrow and pain when he approached me, and I couldn't shake it. I could smell the alcohol seeping out of his pours. I heard the Lord tell me he needed healing. Then someone came and asked him if he could help when he could. It was so uncomfortable, but I couldn't shake it. So, I asked the man if he was in pain. He looked at me crazy and was like, oh yeah, my spine is fractured. So, I told him I believed God wanted to heal him and asked if I could borrow him for another minute. He looked at me, and his eyes lit up. So, I put my hand on his back (in the right spot) and commanded all pain and inflammation to go in the name of Jesus and then commanded his spine to be healed in Jesus's name and asked the Holy Spirit to fill every crack and broken place in his body. And I'm pretty sure he did it! It was like I was looking at a different man. I didn't feel any more pain, only hope and excitement. He introduced himself after and asked my name. I'll check up on him when I get my next supply round. But I'm so pumped I had to push past my stuff and share it with you!" said Cheyanne Mahar.

"Good Morning, Captain. Looking over the past three weeks in my journal has inspired my soul. I'm so thankful to be a Soldier in God's Army! Satan was working on me hard last week, especially on Wednesday. Being able to see that now and then, seeing God's grace bring me through it, is such a blessing! Having eyes that can see how/when I'm being attacked is a tool you have taught me, Captain! Sharing the full situation is too long here. Summation is: Non-believing souls acknowledged God through prayer, the enemy attacked me silently, God spoke to me to let me know, the enemy fought hard to bring me down, and God helped me persevere! Though my body was down recovering from the attack, my spirit was not broken! Praise the Lord! 'The fruit of the spirit is love, joy, and peace.' Three weeks ago, I couldn't have assessed this situation without your knowledge, Captain! Thank you!" said Kimberly Correa.

"Before starting boot camp and church, I was at my all-time lowest. I wanted to know God, but how could he forgive someone like me, an unholy living life, a wrong person? But I walked into your church on a Sunday and got in boot camp with all of y'all, and it's been a game changer. He, in fact, loves and forgives me, and all those things that I thought made my life so hard, just having God as my first priority, has changed all that for me. It's truly changed my life. And the best part is I get to show my 6-year-old about God. He wakes up wanting to listen to "Jesus music" and read his little beginner Bible. I've brought one person to Christ, prayed for multiple, and given bible verses to the ones who struggle just as I was. And that's huge to me because, before boot camp, I couldn't get into the word; I didn't understand it, and now it's a routine of mine, every Morning at 6. It's something I can't function during the day if I don't do it. I'm currently working on my dad, getting him saved, and I won't let up until he walks into that Church with me. Thank you for doing this boot camp. It has truly changed my life and faith."

- Alisha York.

"Satan has definitely put stumbling blocks in my path, but even complete strangers have noticed a change in my actions and the way I'm carrying myself. I believe God used me to help another sister in Christ for the first time last week. He has been empowering me with so much courage and strength. I feel like I can't praise Him enough. Praying yall have a great day!"

- Raine Bynum.

"This boot camp has exposed my heart, mind, and eyes to the daily spiritual battles that surround us. I now realize when they start in my mind. I immediately cease them by pleading for

Jesus's blood, and the battle washes away. The battles come again, but it's so comforting to know that the blood of Jesus is ammo that I will never run out of!! The other thing this camp has done. I now sometimes see people's spiritual battles in their eyes. Honestly, I'm not really sure how to handle this. The only thing I know to do is show them love as Jesus loves. No judgment, just love. I don't see their specific battle. I just see that it's happening when I look in someone's eyes sometimes."

- Tanya Allen.

"I think the biggest testimony that boot camp has given me is to see the importance of putting God first, not waking up and getting on social media first, but waking up and starting your day with God. To wake up at six and go straight to something for God is so important; it'll make all your worries, stress, and hurt truly disappear. I used to wake up every morning with my chest heavy, and almost every morning, I'd wake up crying, but it's been well over a month since I've done either one of those. I wake up happy and eager now, all because of God and boot camp. It taught me that there's a Bible verse somewhere for every single problem you have that will help you and completely change your life. But you must pour your heart into and read it; the Bible is truly amazing! I'm living proof of a lost, broken soul who has been found, which all started with boot camp."

- Alisha York.

"It's been great. I missed a few, but my relationship with God has gone more in-depth since you started this boot camp. I've learned how to see the enemy and fight him better. My faith has grown tremendously, and I want my will to align with his. I understand what it means now to die to myself and pick up my cross daily and follow him. I'm willing to sacrifice myself and my fleshly desires to follow Jesus and help make other followers. I spend so much more time with him that my Bible app is at the top of the list on my screen time when I check it in settings. I've quit smoking weed and drinking alcohol. I want my marriage back. Gods really transformed me, brother. Thank you for everything God does through you. I love you"

- Keith Barton.

"Captain Josh, I would like to thank you for your heart and devotion to God and us, your army. In these six weeks, I learned that I have a calling in God with a choice: to do God's will or my will. God gave us weapons to use against all evil. As a disciple (soldier), I must change my mindset and wear the armor of God 24/7 by taking time to read the Bible, worship with song, memorize the word, and put in my heart. To fast, pray, intercede, and fight for my family, church, and others, as well as my enemies (or those who I feel are my enemies). When I fall out of alignment with God, I stop taking time to secure that armor again. I was reminded of who I am in God. I am useful, loved, blessed, and forgiven. I am a soldier (child) of God! "

- Bernie Rodriguez.

Final Thoughts

We closed out the boot camp during our weekend Celebration Services, a service designed to celebrate everything God has recently been doing in the church. We do baptisms, dedications, new members, testimonials, and anything we can celebrate and get excited about. For this weekend's celebration, we celebrated all of the boot campers who completed boot camp and did commissioning. I had 2 of the boot campers come and share their testimonies of how boot camp had utterly changed their life. Holy Cow, it was so cool.

During the commissioning, I read:

2 Timothy 4:1-5 New Living Translation

4 I solemnly urge you in the presence of God and Christ Jesus, who will someday judge the living and the dead when he comes to set up his Kingdom: 2 Preach the word of God. Be prepared, whether the time is favorable or not. Patiently correct, rebuke, and encourage your people with good teaching.

3 For a time is coming when people will no longer listen to sound and wholesome teaching. They will follow their own desires and will look for teachers who will tell them whatever their itching ears want to hear. 4 They will reject the truth and chase after myths.

5 But you should keep a clear mind in every situation. Don't be afraid of suffering for the Lord. Work at telling others the Good News, and fully carry out the ministry God has given you.

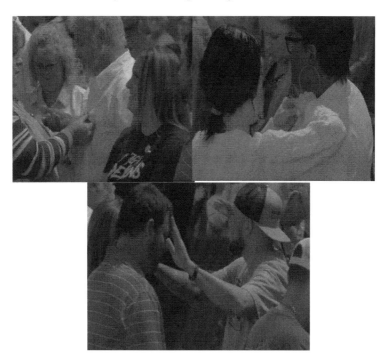

The pinning and prayer of our graduating boot campers

Then, I had my deacons pin them with pins that had the armor of God on them. It is very similar to how the military does pinning. Then my dad came up and prayed over them as the deacons anointed them with oil and commissioned them into the ministry God had for them. We had about 125 people graduate boot camp that day and are absolutely on fire for Jesus. We were doing the work of the ministry. We are planning what is next for the boot campers and our church. We are looking at putting together daily devotions for each series we write and doing a special operations training in 8 weeks that will be all about the special abilities that Paul talks about in 1 Corinthians (Gifts of the Spirit). The goal that day will be to get them filled with the Holy Spirit, have them take a five-fold ministry test, do break-out sessions where they learn about the five-fold ministry apostles, prophets, evangelists, pastors, and teachers, and then end the day with walking in freedom through deliverance.

I hope and pray that this book and series has been as effective in your life, church, or ministry as it has been in ours. I hope and pray that Christians everywhere will wake up and begin to understand that we are living in the middle of a war. We need to step up and fight in that war. We need to understand the war that we are in, learn to use the weapons that God has given us, fight for souls, defend ourselves, our families, and our churches against the enemy, storm the gates of hell, and fight till death.

I hope and pray you will join the army, and together, we can storm the gates of Hell. God Bless you.

- Pastor Joshua Poage